D1545748

RESCUING AIMEE

DELTA FORCE HEROES

SUSAN STOKER

Aimee O'Brien smiled as she walked into Gerry Linkous Elementary School. Several of the students waved at her and some even gave her a hug as they passed. Growing up, she never aspired to be a physical education teacher, but now that she was, she couldn't imagine ever doing anything else.

She probably should be more concerned about cutbacks and losing her job, since many school districts across the country were cutting nonacademic programs, such as physical education and music, but the principal, Jane Allen, had reassured her she was doing everything possible to make sure the nonacademic programs were safe.

"Hey, Aimee."

Aimee looked up into the brown eyes of the one man she couldn't get out of her head. From the first day she'd met him, she'd had the hots for him. Tony Santoro taught first grade and had been hired that year. Aimee had heard several of the teachers complaining about the fact the school district had hired a male teacher, but as soon as they saw him, they changed their tune.

Tony was tall, probably around six feet or so, had long dark hair he kept pulled back in a sexy-as-hell bun, and had a full beard. If Aimee met him in a back alley, and if he was wearing ratty jeans and a leather vest while straddling a Harley, she might have been terrified, but every time she'd seen him, he'd been impeccably dressed. During school hours, he wore slacks and a long-sleeve shirt and tie. He wore a suit jacket every morning, but usually took it off before starting his day.

Every single day.

He never deviated from his professional dress.

The only time she'd seen him wearing anything else was at the school's annual fundraising carnival.

Aimee had to admit that jeans and a polo shirt had never looked sexier. He filled out the worn denim in all the right places, and she could make out the hint of a tattoo on his chest because of the open buttons on his shirt.

Not only was he pleasing to the eye, but he seemed to be a gentle and good guy at the same time. At first, she wasn't sure about him. In her experience, good-looking men seemed to know they were good looking and acted as if they were God's gift to women. Sometimes they surprised you, but more often than not they weren't interested in a long-term relationship.

It was the way Tony treated the kids and fellow teachers that made Aimee want to get to know him better. He had the patience of a saint, never raising his voice to any of the students in his class, even when they were misbehaving. He smiled at all the teachers, was unfailingly polite, and all Aimee could think of was breaking through his courteous demeanor, seeing him lose that iron control of his.

She'd heard he used to be in the military, and she had no idea how he'd gone from the battlefield to the classroom, but obviously he had…and he was good at it. But that nagging curiosity in the back of her head wouldn't quit. She could see the passion just under his calm, controlled appearance, and couldn't help but be intrigued by it. Aimee had had more than one dream about him showing her his true colors.

In bed.

Over and over.

Until she was a puddle of goo on the mussed sheets.

It was becoming an obsession, and it irritated Aimee. She doubted she'd ever catch his eye, not when there were so many other single, beautiful teachers vying for his attention. The other day Aimee had walked in on Marci Ringfield standing inappropriately close to Tony, running her finger up his chest and flirting as if it was an Olympic sport. Aimee had apologized, dropped her gaze, and backed away quickly. That encounter made her realize that regardless of how much she might daydream about sweaty sheets and kinky sex, and no matter that she swore she saw a gleam of interest in his eyes…it probably would never happen.

She wore shorts or sweats to work every day. Her T-shirt and ponytail were standard work attire for her. Playing with the children and running around with them required her to be comfortable. It wasn't as if she could impress Tony with fancy work clothes, but it wasn't just that. She loved playing with the kids, and was usually a sweaty mess by the time Tony's class arrived for gym class every other afternoon. Her plain brown hair, scraped knees, and five-foot-two height made her feel like just another kid around him most of the time.

"Someone forgot their coffee this morning."

His words abruptly brought Aimee out of her thoughts. She had a bad habit of getting lost in her own head at inappropriate times, and she flushed, embarrassed that Tony might have thought she was ignoring him.

"Sorry, I was thinking about my lesson plans for the day, and don't worry, I've consumed more than enough caffeine to get through the morning." The statement about the lesson plans was a small lie, but he didn't have to know that.

They were standing near his classroom door; it was only a few doors down from the gym where Aimee spent most of her time.

"I was wondering if you—"

"Miss O'Brien! Mr. Santoro!" The childish voice screeched at a volume more appropriate for an outside game of tag than a narrow hallway inside an elementary school.

Aimee wondered what Tony was going to ask her, but didn't have time to dwell on it as one of her favorite students, Annie, grabbed her around the waist and gave her a big hug. Aimee knew Annie's mom was a struggling single parent, but she was doing something right because Annie was smart, funny, and always worried about her classmates more than she did about herself.

The little girl was a tomboy down to her toes. She loved getting dirty and had no problem going toe-to-toe with the boys, not only in her class, but those in the older grades as well.

"Good morning, Annie," Aimee told the little girl. "I see you're bright-eyed and bushy-tailed this morning."

"Uh-huh," she responded, letting go of her and turning to give Tony an equally exuberant hug, then turning back to Aimee. "I can't wait until gym today…you said last time we were going to do the obbystick course like the soldiers on the base do and I've been practicing and I can't wait!"

Aimee laughed and ran her hand over Annie's head. "*Obstacle* course, and you're right, we *are* doing that today." Since a lot of the children's parents worked at Fort Hood, the Army base nearby, Aimee decided to make a game of running the kids through a modified obstacle course. So far, the classes that had gone through it seemed to really enjoy it. Aimee got a lot of satisfaction out of making exercise and being healthy fun.

"Yay!" Annie screeched, then waved at them both and tore down the hall toward her classroom.

"Whew, I swear some of the kids make me tired just watching them," Aimee breathed, smiling while watching Annie half run, half skip down the hall to her classroom, forgetting for a moment she'd dreamed about being naked in bed with the man standing next to her.

Tony chuckled. "Agreed. I wish I had half the energy they do sometimes."

Aimee grinned shyly up at Tony, noticing how once again he'd managed to look sexy but respectable at the same time. His white shirt looked as if it'd been freshly ironed that morning, and his tie with the snowman from the movie *Frozen* on it somehow made him look *more* masculine, rather than silly or wimpy. His long hair was in its customary low bun at the back of his head and Aimee swore she could see herself reflected in his shiny shoes.

Rubbing a hand self-consciously on her track pants, knowing she looked as though she just rolled out of bed compared to him, she told him honestly, "You look nice today."

"Thanks." Gesturing to his tie, he said, "I figured in honor of the snowstorm up in Montana today, I'd wear this tie."

"It's cute."

He shrugged a little self-consciously. "Cute. Yeah. You know what, at the end of the day, sometimes I forget I'm wearing some of my more colorful ties, and it's not until the lady at the checkout counter smirks at me that I remember."

Aimee almost reached out and stroked his chest over the tie, but restrained herself just in time. "I like it. Your students love you and love your choice of ties. Every time they come in for gym, I hear all about which one you're wearing that day. You're doing a great job here, Tony."

She swore she saw the man blush, but didn't comment on it. There was no way he didn't know how much his students liked him.

"Thanks." He shrugged. "I wasn't sure I'd be accepted when I first started. You don't see too many male elementary teachers these days. Especially not my age."

"You're what, eighty-seven?" Aimee teased.

"Brat." Tony grinned. "Thirty-two, if you must know."

"Oooh, you're ancient. Almost retirement age."

There was a small pause in their conversation, and Tony just stood there smiling at her, as if he was waiting for something.

"What?" Aimee asked, putting her hands on her hips.

"I told you how old I am, it's your turn."

"Oh no, don't you know it's rude to ask a woman her age?"

"I could guess."

"Good Lord, don't do that. That's worse than asking. I mean, if you guess too high, I'll feel bad because you think I'm an old hag. But if you guess too young, I'll be crushed because you see me as too young for you or something." She hadn't thought about the words coming out of her mouth until his response.

"I don't think you're too young for me, and from what I can see, you're definitely not too old either. In fact, I think you're just about perfect."

Aimee didn't know what to say. Had Tony just told her he was attracted to her? He went on before she could blurt out something embarrassing like, "Yes, please take me to bed and do any wicked thing you want to me."

"I feel comfortable in guessing that you're

twenty-eight." When she didn't say anything, Tony pressed, "Am I right?"

She nodded, but narrowed her eyes at him suspiciously. "Yeah, but was that really a guess? You sounded way too sure of yourself."

He laughed outright, and Aimee couldn't do anything but stare at his mouth. Every time she talked to him, he became more and more attractive.

"You got me. I heard Jane talking to another teacher about how lucky they were to have you here. That you were only twenty-eight, but it was as if you'd been doing this your entire life, even though you just graduated two years ago."

Aimee felt a need to explain for some reason. "When I graduated from high school, I thought I wanted to serve my country and all that." She waved her hand to illustrate *all that*. "I was quickly disillusioned and realized all the rules and regulations that went into military life wasn't for me. I'm more of a free spirit and tend to make decisions on the fly. I didn't particularly like to be told to do something that I felt was the wrong decision. Not to mention my height wasn't exactly conducive for looking tough. I was made fun of more in Basic and at my first duty station than I ever was growing up. So I did my four years, then used my

GI Bill to go to school and get my teaching degree."

"Good for you. The kids love PE. I've never seen anything like it. I would've guessed that most kids hate running around and exercising, especially in today's digital age. But every single student I've talked to thinks you walk on water and they'd happily do suicides until they dropped if you asked."

Aimee felt herself blush, but brushed over his praise. She wasn't comfortable with it, feeling as if she was only doing her job. "Thanks. You were in the Army too, weren't you?" Aimee regretted the question as soon as it left her mouth, because Tony's entire demeanor changed. It was if a curtain fell over his expression, as it turned blank.

"Yeah. I did some time."

Wanting to make it right, but not knowing exactly how, Aimee did what she usually did— jumped in with both feet. "I'm sorry if I brought up some bad memories, but still, thank you for your service. I know a lot of people had it tough…my time in was boring in comparison. I was never deployed and feel kinda like a poser as a result. But seriously, thank you."

Tony ran his hand over his head and shifted

uncomfortably in front of her. "No, *I'm* sorry. That part of my life doesn't hold the best memories for me. I enjoyed the camaraderie and helping people who were simply trying to live their lives."

Aimee tilted her head at him, considering her next words.

"Go on."

"Go on, what?" she asked, furrowing her brow in confusion.

"Ask me whatever it is that's knocking around in that brain of yours."

Aimee laughed a little self-consciously, but asked what she'd been thinking, knowing she probably wouldn't get another opening as good as this one. "How'd you go from there to teaching? I mean, I know how *I* did it, but I don't expect you were mopping up pee from a party the night before in the barracks and decided enough was enough."

She honestly didn't think he was going to answer, classes were going to start soon and they both had prep they had to do, but finally he took a deep breath and looked her in the eye.

"I was in the middle of the most intense firefight I'd ever been in. We were pinned down in the ruins of a building by insurgents. One of my buddies was lying behind me with a bullet hole in his head. He had been talking to me one second, and the next he was dead. Bullets were flying, civilians were screaming, kids were crying…it was absolute chaos. I peeked out from behind the wall, and saw a kid, around ten or eleven, lying in the middle of the road. He was on his back, arms outstretched on either side of him, staring up into nothing. A leather satchel was next to him, with books falling out of it."

Tony sighed and ran a hand through his hair. Aimee almost regretted asking, he was obviously stressed, but it was the relief she saw in his eyes at being able to talk about it that made her nod and put one of her hands on his arm in support.

It seemed to be what he needed to continue. "The kid was on his way home from school and got caught in the middle of a hail of gunfire. He didn't care about the Americans or the political climate. He was going about his day, trying to learn, when his life was cut short. I decided right then and there, if I got out of that fight alive, that I wouldn't reenlist when my time was up. I wanted to atone for that little boy somehow. I wasn't completely sure I wanted to teach, but it seemed to be what I should do.

"I started taking online classes the second I got

back in the States after that deployment. From the first time I stepped foot inside a classroom during my program, I knew it was what I was born to do. I love teaching…seeing a kid's face light up when they finally 'get it' is the most rewarding thing I've ever seen in my life. It won't bring that boy back, I know that, but it helps to know that I'm helping shape kids in some fundamental way. Maybe they'll look back and remember what Mr. Santoro taught them someday." He shrugged a little sheepishly. "Or maybe they'll look back and think I was the biggest dork of a teacher they'd ever had."

"I seriously doubt that." Aimee smiled up at him. She could tell he was being completely honest, and his story was as amazing and awe inspiring as it was heartbreaking. The more she learned about this man, the more she liked him. They'd talked a few times over the last few months, but this was the most…intimate they'd gotten. And it *felt* intimate. Even though they were standing in the middle of a hallway with people all around them, she could tell that Tony seemed to enjoy talking to her. It made her feel a sliver of hope that maybe, over time, he might be interested in more.

The noise level in the hallway rose as more and more children began to arrive. "Thank you for sharing that with me. I was impressed with how well you were doing before, but now that I know a little more about you, I'm even more so." She looked around, then back at Tony. "I have to get going. I have Mrs. Nooncaster's kids this morning…you know how crazy they are," Aimee said with some regret.

"Yeah, good luck with that," Tony told her, the hollow look in his eyes retreating at the change in subject.

"Thanks. You were going to ask me something before Annie interrupted us?" Aimee dared to ask.

"It was nothing," Tony reassured her, not taking the bait.

Aimee was disappointed, but not that surprised. "Okay, I'll see you later then?"

"Yup. I know you've got Mrs. Brown's fourth-grade class before mine today, right?"

"Yeah. She's always late picking them up, but if she takes too long, I'll just get them to help me with your first-graders. Okay?"

"Of course. Whatever you want."

"Whatever I want?" Aimee couldn't help but ask with a gleam in her eye.

Instead of smiling and joking back with her, Tony said in a serious voice, "You're the kind of woman a man would bend over backward to please. See you later."

Aimee stood in the hallway, stunned into silence at Tony's words. He hadn't given her a chance to respond, but she had no idea what she would've said anyway.

Wow. Slowly she smiled. It was going to be a good day.

TWO

By lunchtime, Aimee was exhausted, but in a good way. The obstacle course was a huge hit with the kids. She smiled to herself, remembering little Annie. She'd taken one look at what they would be doing and vibrated with excitement. She was an odd little girl, but not in a bad way. She loved all things "military" and "boy." This obstacle course was right up her alley.

When the forty minutes of PE was over, all the kids were sad and begged to be able to do the course the next time they had gym. Figuring if the kids were happy, and exercising, it was a win-win, so Aimee agreed with no hesitation. Annie had given her a huge hug before leaving the gym, whispering,

"This was the best day *ever*." Moments like that were why Aimee was a teacher.

She usually ate lunch in the gym, stuffing her face between trying to set up for the next class's activity, but since she was using the same obstacle course for all the grades, she didn't have anything to do. Remembering the interested look in Tony's eyes that morning, she decided to take a risk and see if he was eating in the teachers' lounge.

Standing in front of the door, Aimee realized that she probably should've taken the time to make sure she was presentable before coming to lunch. She could feel some of her hair hanging around her face, escaping her ponytail. Putting down her lunch bag to free up her hands, she quickly tore out the scrunchie and re-did it. Looking down at her track pants and T-shirt, she noticed streaks of dirt on her chest and there was a small tear in her pants at the knee.

She'd fallen when she'd lunged to catch one of the kindergartners who'd tripped over a tire. The little boy would've face-planted, but she'd reached him in time. The tires were the hardest part of the course, and she'd learned to stand by just in case someone fell. The little boy wasn't the only one she'd had to rescue that morning, but because he was heavier than the other students, she'd toppled over and had taken the brunt of the fall on her knees.

It was totally worth ruining her pants, but at this very moment, she wished that she looked a bit more put together. Aimee mentally shrugged. Whatever. This was who she was, and she wouldn't apologize for it. It *seemed* as though Tony liked gym-teacher Aimee, so it wasn't as if he was expecting her to waltz into the room wearing a prom dress or something. She was still trying to wrap her mind around the fact that she might, after all, have a chance with Tony, but made a mental note to always be herself. She didn't want to change who she was to try to catch a man's eye. She was just fine the way she was, and if he didn't realize it, it'd be *his* loss, not hers.

Grabbing her lunch bag from the floor, Aimee pushed open the door and smiled at the animated conversation that greeted her. The teachers all seemed to be serious and studious when she spoke to them when they passed off their classes to her, but one-on-one and away from the children, they were sarcastic, loud, and more often than not, hilarious.

Tony was sitting at one of the tables at the back

of the small space, and Marci was sitting next to him. She was leaning toward him with her hand on her chin, elbow on the table. At first glance it looked they were having an intimate conversation, but when Aimee looked closer, she could see Tony was sitting rigid in his seat and was looking down at his lunch, and not at her.

Aimee took one step into the room and saw Tony suddenly stand up and give her a chin lift. Ignoring Marci, who was now almost trying to plant herself in his lap, he called out to Aimee, "Hey, I've been waiting for you. I'm ready, I'll just grab my stuff and be there in a second."

Aimee stood paralyzed for a moment, wondering what in the heck he was talking about. She'd been known to be scatterbrained sometimes, but she knew she'd never forget making plans to be with Tony during lunch.

Never.

No way in hell.

It would've been tattooed on her brain.

She watched as he quickly gathered his uneaten sandwich and chips and stuffed them back into the fabric lunch bag he'd brought with him. It had Elsa from *Frozen* on it, and was most likely a gift from one of his first-graders. The fact that this manly-looking specimen would use it for his lunch was another punch in Aimee's gut. He didn't even look embarrassed to be carrying it either. Damn.

Marci pouted up at him, obviously unhappy their lunch together was being interrupted. Tony leaned down and said something to her. Marci stopped pouting and smiled prettily up at him. She put her hand on his hip, and Tony quickly took a step backward, dislodging her hand but pretending not to notice.

The other teachers in the room watched the little drama playing out, but Aimee couldn't tell what they were thinking. Tony waved at the room in general as he came up to her.

Tony sighed in relief at Aimee's presence. He'd been sitting next to Marci, wondering how in the hell he was going to extricate himself from her clutches, when Aimee walked in. Marci had been getting more and more aggressive in her pursuit of him, but he didn't want anything to do with her. He'd heard the gossip; it was impossible not to hear it, as the other teachers seemed to love to talk. Apparently, Marci had a bet with another one of the fifth-grade teachers that she'd have him in her bed by the end of the school year. Tony didn't know what the bet was for, but he didn't want any part of the pretty-but-she-knew-it teacher.

He much preferred Aimee's understated beauty. She took the girl-next-door to the next level. Tony could usually control his libido and desires, but something about Aimee got to him.

He shook his head and tried to concentrate on getting away from the teachers' lounge without doing something embarrassing, like going down on his knees and thanking her for rescuing him from Marci's grasp.

Aimee didn't usually eat in the teachers' lounge, but Tony took her presence as a sign that he needed to get his head out of his ass and finally ask her out. He'd almost done it that morning before they'd been interrupted by Annie.

But when Aimee had flat-out asked him what he was going to say before Annie came up to them, the time hadn't seemed right. It was ridiculous. He was a grown man, an Army vet, Special Forces at that, and he'd seen way too many horrible things in his life. Why was he hesitating about asking Aimee out?

Bless the woman, when he reached her in the doorway, she didn't contradict him or otherwise make it obvious he'd made up the meeting to get away from Marci. She simply smiled at him and turned around and pushed the door open.

"Ready to go?"

"After you," Tony gestured and held the door open. He tried not to peek at her ass as she walked in front of him, but couldn't help it. She had an ass men would fight wars over.

When the door had shut behind them, she peered up at him mischievously. "Not that I don't want to eat with you…but I'm assuming there's a story behind this lunch meeting that I didn't know we had?"

Tony sighed. "Yeah. Marci won't take a hint that I'm not interested in her."

Aimee nodded as if she knew that was what he was going to say and understood completely. It wasn't as if Marci's pursuit of him was a secret. "I'm not sure *why* you're not interested in her. She's tall, skinny, and blonde. She has big boobs, and she obviously wants you."

Tony stopped in front of the gym and pulled open the door, holding it ajar for Aimee once again. "Honestly? She's so not my type."

He laughed at the blatant look of disbelief Aimee gave him. "Seriously," he defended himself, "she might be pretty, but she knows it. She's spoiled and accustomed to using her looks to have men fall all over her. I've seen her in action. One of her fifth-graders' fathers was upset over something, and she pulled her shirt down a bit and fluttered her eyes at him, and by the time the man left, he had no idea what had happened. Amazingly, she's a good teacher, but I have no desire to get caught in her web."

They walked to the bleachers and sat on the second row, propping their feet up on the first bench and tucking into their lunches.

"So, what is your type then?" Aimee asked seriously. "I thought all guys liked that sort of thing."

Tony's hand halted halfway to his mouth and he turned to Aimee in disbelief. "Are you serious?"

"Well, yeah," Aimee stammered. "I mean, I've seen it over and over again. First in the Army... anytime I went out with friends, the soldiers flocked to the women who were wearing high heels, skimpy clothes, and a ton of makeup. And if they had fake boobs, all the better. They never left the bar alone. Then after, in college, it was the same thing. The girls who went out of their way to be sexy always had boyfriends."

Tony put down his sandwich and turned sideways on his seat toward Aimee. He waited until she looked up at him. She was being completely honest with him, not fishing for compliments or otherwise trying to flirt.

It was crazy.

It was unbelievable.

It was a total turn on.

She had no idea that he'd been drooling over her since the moment he'd met her at the beginning of the school year. Six months of him trying to drop hints and make her *see* that he was interested, and she still had no clue. It should've irritated him, but instead it made him understand that she was a woman who, because she *played* no games, didn't *understand* the games. The best thing he could do was be upfront and honest. He might strike out, but at least she'd know straight off that he was interested in her.

"My type? I don't suppose I have a body type that I'm always attracted to. I've been attracted to chubby women, tall women, short women...I once fell in love with an Indian woman I met when I was stationed overseas. It's not the outward package that interests me, Aimee, it's what inside her that matters to me."

Aimee crossed her arms over her chest and scowled up at him adorably. "Are you telling me that you wouldn't care if a woman weighed six hundred pounds as long as she was a good person?"

"No, not necessarily," he returned immediately. "There's a certain amount of sexual attraction that I need to feel toward a woman before deciding we're compatible for something long term. But that sexual attraction is dependent on me liking her personality." Seeing she wasn't buying it, he switched gears. "Let me give you a concrete example. Let's take Marci. I think we can both agree she's pretty, right?"

Aimee nodded reluctantly.

"Right, so she's good looking, as you said, tall, blonde, and stacked. But she uses people. Parents, the principal, other teachers, probably even the kids if she could. I don't like that. I don't do one-night stands, Aimee. I'm thirty-two, that's not what I want in a relationship."

"No one said you had to marry her. I'm sure she would be glad to date you, even if it didn't end with a forever relationship." Aimee put both hands in the air and finger-quoted the word relationship as she said it. Tony wanted to laugh, but knew they were in the middle of a serious conversation.

"I admit that if I was ten years younger, I probably wouldn't have hesitated. I had my share of one-night stands and screwing any woman who threw herself at me. But, Aimee, that's not me now. I want to find a woman I can talk to. Someone I can eat dinner with and laugh over the funny things that happened to us since we last saw each other. I want her to meet my friends and my family. I want to *like* her. I respect Marci for the teacher she is, but I in no way want to have her on my arm when we meet my friends. She's manipulative, and I can imagine that the second she 'gets' me, she'll be trying to find her next target. She tried to manipulate me into making a move on her in the teachers' lounge before you got there."

"How?"

Seeing the way Aimee frowned when he'd admitted the other woman was trying to get to him made him feel better. She didn't comment on his relationship remark, but he could tell she was pleased with his answer. Tony wasn't sure it was jealousy he was seeing in her eyes when he'd mentioned being with Marci, but he'd work with what he could get. "Just now, she leaned against me reaching for the salt, making sure her tit pressed into my arm. Other instances include how she usually wears enough perfume to choke a horse, thinking it'll turn me on. She even once claimed her car was acting up and asked if I would check it for her at the end of the day."

"Bitch," Aimee murmured under her breath.

Tony smiled, but once again, didn't comment on it. He had a point to make. "You want to know what kind of woman I'm attracted to?" Not giving her a chance to respond, he made his move, wanting Aimee to know without a doubt that he wanted to date her. "Petite women who fit snugly against my side. There's something about the thought of being able to look down at a woman and seeing her rise up on her tiptoes to reach my mouth, that turns me on. I don't usually care about hair color, but long brown hair is sexy as hell, even when it's up in a ponytail." His eyes went to her head, knowing she was watching him.

"I can't help but think about taking it down and seeing it fall against her back, and maybe my own skin."

Aimee opened her mouth to say something, but Tony kept going. He was neck-deep in it now, he might as well go all the way. He'd chickened out that morning, but Marci's actions in the lounge made him realize he needed to suck it up and make a move. If Aimee wasn't interested, she wasn't interested, but he thought he saw something in her eyes that hinted that she was.

"As for clothes, I've never been a fan of high heels. They look painful as all get out and I've seen way too many women roll an ankle wearing them. And while I admit to enjoying and appreciating seeing a woman all dressed up, making an effort for her man, I know that's not a twenty-four/seven reality. I've been around enough females to know they're much more comfortable in sweats and a T-shirt. I'd take comfortable and relaxed over stressed, anxious, and made-up any day. And when I start dating someone, I'll see a lot more of her in comfy clothes than dressed to the nines. If I'm attracted to her while she's dressed down, I know I'll have my socks knocked off when she puts in the effort. And I have no problem letting her know that her effort is *more* than worth it."

Tony took a deep breath, then continued, winding down. "It's like this. If I have filet mignon every day, it gets old. It loses that something special. So when I *do* order it, I appreciate it more and it's a treat. Does that make sense?"

"Did you just compare a dressed-up woman up to a slab of meat?"

Tony chuckled. It figured she'd call him on his

bad choice of words. "I guess I did. It probably wasn't the best analogy, huh? In case you haven't figured this out, in my bumbling way of trying to say it, I'm attracted to *you*, Aimee."

The words lay between them and he saw Aimee swallow hard once. Then twice.

"I don't think I *own* a dress," she finally blurted out.

"I don't care."

Aimee looked away for a long moment, then turned back to him. "I'm attracted to you too."

"Well, whew!" Tony pantomimed wiping his brow. "That makes this a lot less awkward."

She smiled at him and rolled her eyes. "As if I wouldn't be."

"You'd be surprised," Tony told her, pausing to take a bite of his sandwich. He felt much more comfortable now. He'd told her he was attracted to her, and it was out in the open. It was even better that apparently she felt the same, and wasn't afraid to tell him. "The long hair and beard isn't exactly the most popular thing among elementary school teachers these days. Not to mention, have you seen those posts online where they talk about how many germs can be hanging out in facial hair?"

Aimee laughed. "Yeah, although the one about 'glitter beards' seems right up your alley."

"Evil. Glitter is the devil," Tony returned, somehow keeping a straight face. "I wouldn't let anyone, no matter how much I wanted to impress her, get near me with glitter."

"Oh come on, a first-grade teacher is supposed to love that stuff."

"Do you know where I've *found* that devil's invention when I've gotten home after a day of crafts?" He mock shuddered. "It's horrible stuff, thought up by a jilted lover, I'm sure of it."

He loved the giggle that escaped Aimee's mouth. "Seriously though," he continued, "I think you're underestimating the popularity of the beard-and-long-hair thing. I've had women come up to me and want me to seductively toss my hair around and put it on top of my head. I have no clue what that's about. With that being said, though, it does seem to work for some women, and totally turns others off. I've had some women say to my face that I'd be a lot hotter if I cut my hair short."

At her look of disbelief, his eyes went wide and he nodded. "Oh yeah, no lie. They come right up to me, in my personal space; and once, while I was eating at a restaurant with two of my buddies, a woman told me we'd be the three musketeers of hotness if only I got rid of the 'nasty long-hair shit'."

"She must have been mentally ill," Aimee muttered. Then asked louder, "Why *do* you keep it long? All the military guys I know had short hair."

Tony shrugged. "I'm essentially lazy."

"Now *that* I don't believe," Aimee protested. "No one who teaches first grade can be lazy. It's not in your DNA."

"Lazy might not be the best word," he conceded. "I just got used to it being this way when I was in the Special Forces. Helped me blend in over in the Middle East. In some ways, it's easier to hide behind it now than to cut and shave it off."

"I didn't know you were in the Special Forces," Aimee said gently. Out of all the women he'd told since he'd gotten out, Tony knew Aimee understood more than most what that meant.

"I was." He didn't elaborate.

Aimee put her hand on his knee and squeezed briefly. "That puts the situation you told me about earlier today in a whole different light now. Thank you for all that you did. I know you can't talk about it, but seriously, thank you."

Tony swallowed the lump that formed in his

throat. He'd seen and done some horrible things that he'd never tell another soul as long as he lived. He hadn't lied to her earlier, that little boy lying dead in the middle of the road with his school books strewn around him had been the catalyst to make him want to change his life, but it certainly hadn't been the worst thing he'd seen. Not even close. He'd gotten out because he couldn't handle the nightmares and violence he saw long after the missions ended. He changed the subject. "So…now that it's out in the open that we like each other… would you like to go out sometime?"

"Yes."

He smiled at her, loving that she didn't play games.

She continued, clarifying her answer. "As long as you don't expect me to put on a dress. I wasn't lying when I said I didn't own one. I think I might have a pair of nice jeans I can pull out from the bottom of my closet, but anything more is pushing it."

"Deal. I was thinking dinner at a steak house sometime soon."

"In the mood for filet mignon, huh?"

Tony burst out with a laugh. "I walked right into that one, didn't I? There's nothing wrong with filet mignon every now and then, but as I told you…I'm perfectly happy with hamburger every day of my life."

"I think you'd better stop while you're ahead," she told him, smiling to let him know she wasn't offended in the least.

Feeling on top of the world, Tony ate some chips and changed the subject. She'd said yes. He'd figure out the details later. It was enough to know they'd be going on a date, soon. "So, an obstacle course huh? How's it work?"

Aimee settled back onto her elbows next to him, looking out on the gym floor. Pointing as she spoke, she explained, "They start with the tires, getting through them how they can based on their age: hopping, walking, jumping, whatever. Then they head to the cones and weave in and out of them. Next is the balance beam, I borrowed it from a friend across town who runs a gymnastics club. It's only three inches off the ground, but I told the kids to pretend they were crossing a stream and so far they've loved it. There's a sit-up and push-up station, then they have to pull weights twenty feet, run three suicides, and finish up by climbing up and over the giant mound of mats."

"It looks fun."

"It *is* fun," Aimee returned. "If you weren't all buttoned up and stuffy looking, I might challenge you."

"You think you can beat me?"

"No, but I *do* think I could give you a run for your money…especially if you gave me a ten-second head start."

"Deal. Some day this week after school we'll do it."

"Really?"

"Really."

Aimee tilted her head and looked at him, obviously trying to gauge if he was telling the truth or not. Finally she just shrugged. "Okay."

"But we have to bet something on it."

"I didn't think, with the rumors going around, that you'd want to bet. But I'm game. What're the stakes?"

Tony ignored her snarkiness regarding the bet about him and Marci and pretended to think about it, but he knew just want he wanted. "A kiss."

Aimee's eyebrows went up and she answered him in an over-the-top English accent. "Why, sir, are you trying to ruin me, you scoundrel?"

"Yes."

They both laughed.

Dropping the accent, she agreed. "It's a deal. If you win, you get a kiss. If I win, you'll clean the entire gym floor."

"Ouch, woman. I was hoping you might want to claim a kiss if you won as well."

She leaned into him and whispered, "I'm just giving you more incentive to win."

Tony couldn't remember a time with a woman that he'd had more fun. Aimee was down-to-earth, funny, and he admired her. She might only be five-two, but she had the personality of one of his drill sergeants back when he'd joined the Army. That woman was a bit taller than Aimee, but she was the scariest sergeant in the bunch, and not one of the men ever wanted to cross her. "Today after work?"

"Do you have different clothes?"

"Damn."

Their banter was interrupted by the sound of the end-of-lunch bell. They looked at each other for a long moment.

"I've enjoyed this," Aimee told him, completely candidly.

"Me too. I'm looking forward to our date."

Aimee nodded. "I'll see you in an hour?"

"Yup. Good luck with Mrs. Brown's class."

"Thanks, I might need it. They're always riled up right after lunch."

"I'll see if I can't get my kids here a bit early. Since she's usually late picking them up, it's good for the younger kids to play with the older ones every now and then."

"Cool. And I think the fourth-graders really enjoy being the 'experts' with your crew."

Tony put the empty bags from his lunch into his *Frozen* lunch sack and stood, holding out his hand for Aimee. She grabbed it and stepped down from the bleachers. He leaned down a couple inches and said softly, "Thanks for lunch, and for agreeing to go out with me."

Aimee blushed, but nodded in agreement. She stood up on her tiptoes; Tony had no idea if she was doing it because he'd mentioned it earlier or not, but she brushed her lips against his cheek, above his beard. "Me too."

He took a step back from her, wanting nothing more than to grab her in his arms until her feet weren't touching the ground and ravish her mouth, but knowing it wasn't the time or the place. "See you later, Aimee."

"Bye, Tony."

Tony walked out of the gym smiling from ear to

ear. He didn't think he could've ever been thankful to Marci for anything, but her uncomfortable flirting was the impetus he'd needed to get his butt in gear and ask Aimee out. He walked toward his class, trying to think about what they might do after their steakhouse dinner. He wanted to impress her and find something she'd enjoy. He knew it would need to be something different, something he hadn't done with any other woman. Aimee was one of a kind and he wanted her to know it. He'd have to think more on it, but was thankful for the chance. Something in his gut told him she was the woman for him, he wasn't going to screw it up now.

THREE

J ones Thompson sat across from his good
friend, Cormac "Fletch" Fletcher. They were
hanging out in Ruby's Cafeteria in Killeen,
Texas, after finishing their meal. Jones had come to
Texas for a conference on hostage negotiation from
Roanoke, Virginia, where he lived. The meeting
was held in Austin, but when it was over, he reached
out to Fletch, eager to spend some time with the
friend he hadn't seen in way too long.

"How's civilian life treatin' ya?" Fletch asked,
leaning back in his chair.

"Overall, good."

"I know you were more than ready to get out…
was it the right decision?"

Jones thought about his answer. He'd worked

with Fletch while he was in the Army. They were both Delta Force, although Jones was stationed out of Colorado instead of Texas. Their missions frequently required more than one team, so they'd fought side by side many times over the last few years.

The stress of the missions had gotten to Jones though, and he knew he had to get out, or have a greater-than-average chance of becoming one of the homeless veterans on the street who couldn't hold down a job or live a normal life because of the shit going on in his head.

"It was. Thank God for Tex. If it wasn't for him putting me in contact with a former SEAL turned cop in Roanoke, I'd probably be camped out in the apartment over your garage being a bum."

Both men laughed at the mental imagery Jones's words evoked.

"First of all, it's already rented, so you'd be out of luck, but I have no doubt you would've found something that fit you. This guy—he's good?" Fletch asked, the skepticism he was trying to keep out of his voice leaking through anyway.

Jones nodded. "Hopefully you found a good renter this time. Remember that one guy who thought he could grow pot in the apartment without you knowing?" They both chuckled at the memory.

"What a douche. This time I think I've got a good one. Woman and her kid. They shouldn't cause too many problems. And I can pretty much guarantee she won't be trying to start up a drug business," Fletch said wryly.

"Good. Glad to hear it. And to answer your question, yeah, Joker is good. I had my doubts at first as well. I mean, Tex vouched for him. That in itself went a long way toward assuaging my concerns about him. But he's only hired former military men and women and I truly feel as if I'm making a difference. I've learned a lot about hostage negotiation and interrogation from Joker and was thrilled to be able to come up here for more advanced training."

Fletch chuckled. "Yeah, us Deltas tend to blow in first, and negotiate later."

Jones laughed with his friend. "Yeah, I've been accused of being a bit heavy-handed myself sometimes."

"You got a case waiting for you when you go back to Virginia?"

"There are a few things in the queue, but generally we work bigger investigations…things like terrorist threats and hostage situations."

"No domestic disputes and checking into allegations of affairs?" Fletch joked.

"Fuck no. Joker doesn't waste our time with that shit. There are enough private investigators in Virginia who can do that stuff. Joker wants to make a difference in the world, not deal with men who can't keep their dicks in their pants or women who want a sugar daddy on the side. I enjoy working for him. It's kinda like working on the teams."

"How so?" Fletch asked with genuine curiosity.

"When I was in Delta, we worked as a team. All information was shared, we moved as one, we had one objective, and we conquered that objective. One man wasn't better or more important than the others. That's how it is with Joker and the men and women I work with. No one is trying to outdo the other, no one wants accolades over someone else as sometimes happens with private security groups. It's a true team. Our meetings can run through the night, but no one bitches about the long hours, no one complains about overtime. It's just what we do."

"I'm happy for you man, seriously. I know we've all been through hell, but we could all see what it was doing to you. Ghost, Coach, Blade, and all the others on my team saw it just as clearly as your own teammates did. You're a good man, and anytime you need backup, I hope you know all you have to do is ask and we're there for you."

"I appreciate that," Jones told his friend. "I feel like I'm just where I need to be. I don't know why, or how, but things are working out for me and I'm fucking thrilled."

With that, Jones and Fletch stood up, ready to go, and shook hands.

As they headed out to the parking lot, Fletch asked, "You leaving today?"

"Nope. I'm staying the night here in Killeen, then heading back to Austin to catch my plane back to Virginia in the morning."

"Perfect timing. I'm having a get-together at my house with the team tonight, I hope you'll come."

"Wouldn't miss it," Jones reassured his buddy. "I can't wait to catch up with everyone—and did I hear right that Ghost is in a serious relationship now?"

Fletch smiled. "Hard to believe, but yup. He met Rayne a while ago, but they hooked back up when he rescued her in that Egypt thing."

"Lucky dog," was Jones's response. "I'm not

ready to settle down yet, but I admire anyone on the teams that can make it work. They *are* making it work, right?"

"Oh yeah. She's a lot of fun and brings a whole new dynamic to the group."

"Ghost doesn't have any problem concentrating on missions?"

"Nope. It actually seems to have made him more alert and focused. Guess it's the whole, he-wants-to-get-home-to-his-woman thing."

Both men chuckled.

"Anyway, I'll text you my address. We're putting the steaks on the grill around six-thirty, but you can come anytime."

"Will do," Jones told Fletch. "I appreciate the offer. Steaks sound much more appetizing than the fast food I was planning on grabbing later."

They shook hands next to Jones's nondescript rental car. "It's great to catch up, Jones. Seriously. You look good."

"Thanks. I *feel* good. Virginia has been healthy for me."

"See you tonight," Fletch said, slapping him on the back.

"Later," Jones returned. As he drove toward his hotel, Jones thought about how lucky he was to have a job he enjoyed while still retaining the friendship of the men he'd met during his time in the Army. It seemed that even though he'd been through a lot of shit in his life, he managed to be at the right place at the right time, and he knew the right people at the right time.

FOUR

Aimee swore she smiled nonstop throughout the next hour thinking about her lunch with Tony. In a million years, she never would've been able to guess that not only would the man she'd been secretly drooling over for months seem to like her back, but he'd ask her out on a date as well. There was no way, when they got around to it, that she'd beat him on her little obstacle course. First, he was obviously still in great shape, and second, because she wanted that kiss more than she wanted to win, and that was saying something, since she had always been über competitive.

Mrs. Brown might be interesting to work with—some days she was Miss Congeniality, and others she was Mrs. Grouchy Pants—but her class was amazingly fun to teach. Old enough to not follow blindly what someone in a position of authority did, but young enough that they still wanted to please her and they weren't afraid to cut loose and have fun. They had loved the course she'd set up.

The weights they had to drag were heavier than what the younger kids used, and they were required to do more sit-ups and pull-ups, but overall the course was the same. Since the older students were faster at it, everyone got to go through it several times. Aimee had races, and gladly timed every single student, happy when no one seemed disgruntled when they were beaten by a classmate.

All in all, the thirty minutes had been perfect. Now the anticipation was kicking in…Tony should be by with his class any minute now.

Just as she had the thought, she saw him standing at the door to the gym, his class most likely lined up in the hallway, waiting for permission to enter. She blew her whistle to get the fourth-graders' attention.

"Gather 'round everyone, come here." When the twenty or so kids were all in a circle around her, Aimee squatted down and told them what the plan was. "For the last ten minutes of class, Mr. Santoro has brought his first-graders to join us. I want you all to buddy up with them. Everyone is responsible for one of his students. Since you're older, I want you to show them how to go through the obstacle course. Remember to make it fun and remember that they're littler than you. I'll go and switch out the weights so they're lighter, and please only make them do one or two sit-ups and push-ups. This isn't the Marines. Okay? Any questions?" When no one raised their hand, Aimee motioned to Tony and he led his class inside the gym.

"Okay, go pick a buddy and line up behind the tires. Double up with each other when there are no more first-graders. Go one at a time. When someone is finished with the tires, the next person can start. Don't bunch up, leave plenty of room. And go!"

The fourth-graders raced off, eager to show the course to the younger children. Aimee tried to have the different grades interact as much as possible, wanting to increase the feeling of camaraderie at the small school.

They watched the kids playing for a while until Tony leaned over and whispered, "You haven't changed your mind, have you?"

"About going on a date with you?" When he

nodded, Aimee was quick to reassure him. "No. Have you?"

"Nope."

"Good, 'cos I've been looking forward to it."

He smiled at her, but it quickly disappeared when they heard an odd sound. Tony's head cocked and they both froze. The kids continued to shriek and laugh as they went through the obstacle course.

"Did you hear that?" Tony asked her.

Aimee nodded. "Yeah, I think so, but what was it?"

Tony opened his mouth to speak when the sound came again. This time, both Army veterans had no problem discerning what the sound was.

"Holy shit," Aimee whispered. Both adults stood stock still for half a second before springing into action. Amazingly, it was as if they'd done this before; they worked in sync to get the students to safety.

Tony ran toward the doors to the gym, while Aimee ran toward the children closest to the doors. She didn't dare risk using her whistle to get the attention of the thirty-six or so children in the room. She took the arms of two students and hissed under her breath to the others nearby. "Quickly, everyone to the other side of the gym where the lockers are. Come on, *now*."

The kids must have heard the urgency in her voice, because they didn't even complain that their playtime was being interrupted.

"John, Mark, please help me round up the rest of the kids," Aimee asked two of the fourth-graders. They immediately nodded and ran to the end of the obstacle course to corral those children to where she wanted them.

Aimee risked a glance up at Tony. He was standing at the doors, trying to figure out how they locked. Pushing a child toward the others, Aimee took the time to run over to Tony.

"They don't lock," she told him breathlessly.

"What?"

"They don't lock," Aimee repeated. "I mean, they do, but I use a chain and a padlock when I leave for the day. They're in my office in the locker room."

"Dammit."

Aimee nodded, understanding his angst. If the doors couldn't lock, they were sitting ducks for anyone who wanted to come inside. Tony put his hand on her shoulder for a moment and looked down at her. "You know what we're dealing with?"

"No," Aimee returned immediately. "But I do know those were gunshots. I'd recognize them anywhere." She took a long look at Tony's face. He was a bit pale, and she could see he was gritting his teeth. "Are you okay? Is this bringing back bad memories?"

"Shit, you're too damn observant. No, this isn't bringing back good thoughts, but I'm fine. We need to protect these kids."

"Yeah." Aimee spun to head back across the gym floor toward the kids, who were now gathered together looking confused. She grabbed Tony's hand and held on as they crossed the gym floor to get to the students.

She kept her voice low as she plotted with Tony, but the urgency came through loud and clear. "We need to treat this like a game. A serious game, but a game, nonetheless. We need to hide them. I don't know if whoever is shooting will make it here or not, but we have to assume they will."

"Where are you gonna hide them? There aren't too many places in here," Tony asked, looking around as they hurried toward the children who appeared extremely worried now. He kept his hand in hers and held on tight.

"In the lockers. It's not ideal, but they're big. I

think we can get two kids in each," Aimee told Tony quickly. They'd reached the children by that time and she didn't bother wasting any time seeing if he agreed with her or not. It was a moot point. There literally was no other place to hide all the kids. They couldn't sneak them out of the gym and it had to be done now.

"Okay kids, here's the deal," Aimee told the frightened students. "There are bad guys in the school, and we need to play hide-and-seek so they can't find us. Remember how we had that police guy come and talk to everyone earlier this year, and he told us all what to do in case of an emergency? It's time to put into practice what you learned that day. I want you to stay with your buddy, and each pair is going to hide inside a locker. You can't make any noise. Not at all. Understand?"

Just then, gunshots sounded again, closer this time. The students obviously heard them, because their eyes got big and some of the younger children started to cry.

Aimee knew this wasn't ideal. There was no way the kids could deal with this like they needed to, but she didn't have time to second guess her decision or to try to reassure them further. It sucked, but it was for their own good. She just hoped they didn't turn out to be degenerates later in life because of the memory of being shut inside a small space while they were scared. Better them scared inside the lockers, and staying undetected, than facing down a lunatic, or lunatics, with a gun and dying in a hail of gunfire.

"Come on, in you go." Aimee wished she could take more time to comfort the kids, but by the sounds of the shots, they didn't have any extra time. She went down the line, shutting two kids into each locker. They had to stand, and it was a tight fit, but the important thing was that they *did* fit. Tony's students were obviously scared, but the older students were taking their job of looking after the younger kid entrusted to their care seriously, and it was helping both groups deal with the terrifying situation. Most had their arms around each other before they were shut inside the lockers.

She noticed that Tony listened to her instructions before helping secure the students. She tried to give each pair a pep talk, with last-minute instructions, before closing the locker door on them.

"You're being very brave and I'm so proud of you both. No matter what you hear, do not make a sound. Don't bang on the door, try not to sneeze or cough. You can cry, but not too loudly. This will be a great trick we play on the bad guys, yeah? I'll come and let you out when we've won. I promise not to leave you in here a second longer than you need to be. Okay?"

Every pair of kids looked up at her with trusting eyes and nodded seriously. Aimee's heart almost broke when a little girl named Shamekia looked up at her with tears and snot running down her face and whispered, "Miss O'Brien, is Mr. Santoro gonna get rid of the bad guys?"

She controlled herself, barely, and whispered back, "Of course he is, sweetie, just be quiet like a mouse and before you know it, Mr. Santoro and I will be letting you out. Okay?"

The little girl nodded solemnly, taking Aimee at her word. She was a trusted adult and Shamekia, and all the other kids, had the utmost faith that their teachers would make this right for them.

Aimee wished there was an outside door or window she could usher the kids out of, as the officers who ran the active-shooter training suggested, but the locker-rooms only led to the hallway, which seemed to be a dangerous exit point when she didn't know exactly what was happening outside the gym or how many shooters there were. When Aimee closed the locker door on the last the pair of children—thank God a kid was absent so they had an even number—she turned to stare at Tony.

He looked just as shell-shocked as she was. "Come on, let's get away from the lockers," Tony ordered, holding out his hand. "We don't want to give their location away to anyone who might come in here. And if we're standing here guarding them, that's exactly what we'll do."

Aimee didn't even hesitate. She grabbed hold of his hand again and allowed him to tow her across the room to the bleachers. They stood next to the bottom row and waited, hands still clenched together, facing the doors.

"Do you think we should hide or try to hold the doors shut?" Aimee whispered.

Tony shook his head. "Unfortunately, no. If someone comes tries to come in, I don't think we could necessarily hold the doors shut and make whoever it is think they're locked. And if someone does come in here, we don't want him, or her or them, to get nosy and start looking around."

"But if we're not visible, and neither are the kids, maybe he'll take one look inside and figure the gym is empty," Aimee argued, playing Devil's Advocate.

"Maybe, but are you willing to bet those kids' lives and take that chance?"

Aimee sighed, knowing Tony was right. "No."

He turned to her and pulled her into his embrace, obviously needing the intimate contact. They stood there silent for a beat before Tony said, "You did good, Aimee. You didn't hesitate to take action. You made a decision and went with it. I can see now why you didn't do more than four years in the Army. I bet you were a crap enlisted soldier, but you would've made a good officer."

"I'm scared," Aimee admitted, not responding to his compliment, too freaked out by what they'd done with the students and the unknown situation they were in.

"I know, believe it or not, I am too. But you pushed through it and you still did what had to be done." He eased back and put his finger under her chin so she had to look at him. "I've seen career soldiers who haven't acted as well as you have under pressure. I'm so damn proud of you, I can't even tell you. I've been attracted to you for months, and you've just proven that what I thought about you has been right. Aimee, I'm going to do what I can to make sure we all get out of this. All right?"

"I'm not ready to die."

"Neither am I. I didn't live through all those missions to die this way. We'll do what we can to help each other and get through this. Yeah?"

Aimee had just nodded when the door to the gym burst open and a man wearing a long black coat, holding two handguns, burst inside the gym as if the hounds of hell were on his heels.

FIVE

Jones was relaxing in his hotel room, hands behind his head, stretched out on the bed, not paying any attention to the show on the television but liking the background noise, when his cell rang. Reaching over to the bedside table, he picked it up and answered.

"Jones."

"It's Tex. There's a situation. You're still in Killeen, right?"

Jones sat up straight on the bed, knowing if Tex was calling him and getting right to the point, something big was happening. "Yes. What's up?"

"Active shooter at Gerry Linkous Elementary School, on Fourth and Main. Reports are that there's only one, but information is sketchy."

"I'm on my way," Jones told Tex without hesitation, already moving around his hotel room, collecting his pistol and identification. "Who should I report to?"

"I've been in communication with a Captain May. It's a long story of how I know about what's going down there, but it involves a buddy who lives in San Antonio who used to be a Delta. I worked with him on a joint-taskforce case. A former Navy officer crossed state lines and fled to Florida after committing a crime there in Texas. Anyway, I told him last week that you'd be in the area at the conference and he knew it was a long shot, but he called to see if you were still around. I offered up your services if they were needed. He's expecting you at the scene. I'm not sure there'll be a chance for you to negotiate...typically the shooter is killed in situations like these, or the locals have their own negotiator, but he's happy to have you there just in case."

"Ten-four," Jones told Tex, unlocking his car door, his mind already going through scenarios and what he should say to gain the shooter's trust to try to convince him to give himself up without hurting anyone if he got the chance. The things he'd learned while at the conference the last few days whirled through his brain.

"The captain has also called the Army base. I wouldn't be surprised to see Ghost and his team there at some point either," Tex told Jones, referring to their Delta Force friends.

Jones nodded in relief. Having the Delta Force team on scene was a good thing. They most likely had more experience with this sort of thing than the local authorities. No one would know they were Delta Force, all Special Forces operatives were required to be tight-lipped about their involvement in the teams, but Jones knew if needed, they'd step up to the plate.

"Good. I had lunch with Fletch earlier today. They know I'm in the area and I'll be sure to hook up with them as soon as I talk with the captain."

"I fucking hate assholes who think it's okay to kill innocent civilians. But there's a special place in hell for people who choose a school full of little kids to make whatever asinine statement they feel they need to make," Tex growled.

"Agreed."

"Take this bastard down, Jones."

"Without a doubt. I'll be in touch."

"I'll be standing by."

The connection was cut as Tex hung up without another word. Jones was used to his friend's abrupt mannerisms, and didn't take offense. He pulled out of the hotel's parking lot and headed as fast as he dared to the area of the elementary school, hoping his Delta friends would be there waiting. If negotiation didn't work, Jones knew Fletch and the others would take care of the shooter one way or another.

SIX

Not giving the shooter time to do anything, Tony stepped away from, and in front of, Aimee, and held up his hands, showing the man he was unarmed. "Don't shoot. We're unarmed."

It was as if Tony hadn't spoken. The man raised a pistol and shot toward them and Tony swore as one of the bullets grazed his arm. Ignoring the pain from the flesh wound, he turned and grabbed Aimee, taking them both to the ground and covering their heads. They could've run, but he figured that would definitely provoke the man to shoot them. They were sitting ducks on the floor in front of him, but it seemed a better option than further provoking the man's need to kill by sprinting away. The situation was precarious and he knew it would take a miracle for either of them to get out alive.

Tony heard the click of the man's gun, indicating it was either out of bullets or had jammed. He waited for the other gun to go off, but it didn't for whatever reason. Temporary miracle delivered.

"Why are you doing this?" Aimee asked, her voice high and stressed, but steady as she looked over at the man from her position on the floor with Tony.

"Why?" the gunman repeated. "Why not?" he said, concentrating on the handgun, trying to reload it. "Maybe I'm Muslim. Maybe I'm doing it because 'hashtag all lives matter.' Maybe it's because I was abused as a child. Maybe the President told me to do it, or because one of the many voices in my head ordered me to. Maybe I'm working with ISIS or I'm a Democrat or Republican. Or maybe I just want to fucking kill people. Does it matter?" His voice had steadily risen in agitation as he spat out his diatribe, but at the end, he finished messing with the weapon that had jammed and pointed it, and the one in his other hand, at them again and demanded, "Where are the kids?"

"What kids?" Aimee asked, trying to sound sincere.

"There should be kids in here," the man grumbled.

"They were," Aimee ventured, "but their teacher picked them up early and I have a planning period now." She tried to sound as earnest as possible, but wasn't sure how successful she was.

"So why is Paul Bunyon here?" the gunman asked astutely, jerking his chin in Tony's direction.

"We're dating. My class is at music and I came down here to spend some time with her," Tony explained quickly.

The gunman laughed as if it was the funniest thing he'd ever heard in his life. "Oh that's rich. Good to see fraternization in the ranks is still alive and kicking. Sorry I interrupted your pussy time," he sneered.

All three turned toward the door, hearing a commotion outside.

"Lock these doors," the gunman ordered, gesturing to the doors while backing away from them, farther into the center of the large room.

Tony and Aimee stood up slowly, but didn't move toward the entrance to the gym. "They don't lock." Aimee repeated the explanation she'd told

Tony earlier. "The school board decided it was too dangerous to have them able to be locked."

"Fucking hell," the man swore.

Tony tried to ignore the wound on his arm, which was slowly oozing blood. Aimee had noticed, of course, and had her hand clamped down over it, trying to staunch the blood flow. It hurt like fuck, but he'd been injured much worse in his previous job.

He fell in love with Aimee at that exact moment. There they were, their lives on the line, the man could shoot them any second, but she still had the presence of mind to put her hand over his arm and try to stop the bleeding. She wasn't freaking out, wasn't crying. He had no doubt she was as scared as she'd admitted earlier, but she was keeping her cool. For a former Special Forces guy who was dealing with a slight case of PTSD, she was a perfect fit for him and a small miracle.

Tony's resolution to get them out of this situation solidified even more. There was no way either of them could die before he found out what her lips felt like on his. What she felt like under him, skin-to-skin. He mentally sent a quick prayer up, asking God to look over both of them, so they had a chance to see where a relationship could go.

Tony looked over at the shooter. For some reason the young man had stopped spraying bullets, and while it was dangerous for them to stay in the gym with the kids hiding yards from where the shooter was, Tony was still grateful bullets were no longer flying. The last thing he wanted was a stray bullet piercing one of the lockers and wounding, or killing, one of the students.

Tony tried to memorize everything about him just in case he managed to get away, as unlikely as that might be. The man was Caucasian, looked like he was in his mid-twenties, and, honestly, was pretty clean-cut looking. Nothing about him stood out, except for the long black coat in the Texas heat. He wasn't declaring his allegiance to Allah, wasn't yelling anything that could give a reason as to why he'd walked into an elementary school and started shooting. Tony wanted to know why he was doing it, but right this second, the whys didn't matter. Getting out alive did.

The man strode over to where Tony and Aimee were, shoved one of his guns into his waistband at the small of his back and, keeping his other pistol aimed at Tony, pulled Aimee toward him by her ponytail, saying, "I'm not going to be shot by some dumb local cops. I'm getting out of here."

Aimee squeaked in pain as she was forced to her feet to walk backward.

"What's your name?" Tony asked suddenly, standing as the man pulled Aimee away from him, wanting to try to connect with this man in some way. He'd wanted to keep hold of Aimee—the last thing he wanted was for her to be in the man's clutches—but playing tug-of-war with Aimee's life wasn't high on his list of things to do.

"Mohammad."

"No, it's not." Tony couldn't keep the irritation out of his voice. "Cut the shit. You're no more a Mohammad than I am. If you're gonna kill me and my girlfriend, at least be honest and tell us your real name and reason for doing this." For a moment, Tony thought he'd gone too far, that the guy was going to shoot both him and Aimee right then and there, but miraculously, the shooter seemed to approve of his straightforward skepticism.

"It's Bill."

"I'm Tony, and that's Aimee," Tony told him, trying to humanize them to the guy who, at the moment, had the power to decide if they were going to live or die.

"I don't fucking care what your names are, you're gonna get me out of here." Bill waved the gun in Tony's direction and shifted until he had a hold of Aimee with an arm around her neck. Because she was shorter than he was by quite a bit, he had to lean over to accomplish it.

Tony met Aimee's eyes. She looked scared, but also pissed, and that was good. Her eyes were wide and her teeth clenched. Her hair was falling out of the ponytail Bill had recently let go of. If she'd been only terrified, she wouldn't be able to think clearly, but he should've known better. She was a soldier, just like he was. She'd proven herself capable to him more than once, he just had to wait for the perfect time to act. The thought ran through his mind that if the gun had jammed once, it could again. He just hoped it wasn't after a bullet had gone through either one of their skulls.

Aimee's hands had moved up to the arm around her throat, and Tony could tell she was aware of just how close her own hand was to the shooter's by the way her eyes flicked to it, then back to him. She might not be able to grab hold of it and use it, but she could at least hold it away from her head…or his. It wasn't a lot, but it was something. He couldn't communicate anything to her without Bill hearing, but he hoped she remembered some of her training from Basic. Close-combat fighting had been covered, miraculously including a situation just like this one.

Tony listened carefully as Bill was busy mumbling under his breath. He didn't hear anything from the other side of the room where they'd stashed the children. The last thing he wanted was Bill to discover they were there and to have thirty-six vulnerable hostages. He knew without a doubt that if Bill threatened one of the kids, both he and Aimee would do whatever he wanted without a fight. They had a much better chance of getting out of this situation without the students being involved. He hoped their luck would hold.

The school was strangely quiet. Tony had no idea if Bill had shot anyone before reaching the gym; it was likely, but there were no screams, no yelling, and he hadn't heard any sirens either.

"How many people did you shoot before you got here?" Tony dared to ask Bill, as if they were standing around at a barbeque shooting the shit.

"Don't know," Bill grunted in response. "Why do you care? You should be worrying about you and your girlfriend here."

"I *do* care about us," he agreed immediately.

"But I'm also concerned about my students, and friends who teach here."

"If you must know, I have no idea," Bill told him candidly. "I just started shooting when I first walked in. I think there were a few people who went down there. By the time I got to the hallway though, most of the doors were locked. Fucking assholes."

Tony breathed a small sigh of relief. Their training on active shooters seemed to have done some good. Along with the local officers speaking to the students, the principal, Jane Allen, had hired a former FBI agent to come to the school during one of the teachers' in-service days to go over protocol for what they should do to "shelter in place." Instructions included locking the classroom doors, piling as many desks up against the door as possible, closing and locking the windows, and huddling together away from both the door and windows, where stray bullets could cause damage.

Having fewer victims to shoot could account for Bill's irritation at the moment. Tony frantically thought through what his next move should be. He was more than aware that every word out of his mouth could either help get them out of the situation, or incite Bill to shoot them both in cold blood.

He'd had basic negotiation classes while in Delta Force, but he'd never had to use anything he'd learned.

Tony had faced death plenty of times during his stint in the military, but this was different. It wasn't just him or his trained team of Army Delta Force operatives...it was *Aimee's* life on the line too. That made all the difference in the world.

Bill had stopped moving as he answered Tony's questions, but he didn't want him to suddenly remember what he'd been doing before he'd been distracted.

A bead of sweat made its way down the small of Tony's back. The stakes had never been higher. "It's hot in here, can I undo my tie?" Tony asked Bill, trying to make the man think he was in charge.

"I don't give a shit, but don't get any ideas that you're gonna be tying me up with that pansy-ass cartoon tie or something."

Tony didn't respond to the taunt, merely released the knot on the tie and pulled it free, stuffing it in his pocket. He unbuttoned a few buttons of his white dress shirt, breathing a bit easier. It had taken him a while to get used to wearing both dress shirts and ties, but it always felt good when he could take them off at home and put on clothes he was more comfortable in. He'd been jealous more than once that Aimee could wear sweats or track pants and T-shirts to work.

"It'd be easier to get out of here if you ditched us and snuck out one of the back doors to the building, you know," Tony said as nonchalantly as he could.

"Too late," Bill stated without much emotion in his words. "Cops have the place surrounded. The only way I'm getting out of here is with you two assholes paving my way."

Tony opened his mouth to respond when a voice rang out through the gym over the loudspeakers. They heard it echoing through the hallway outside the cavernous room as well.

"My name is Jones. We have the building surrounded. Come out with your hands up."

Tony sighed in relief. They weren't out of the woods yet, but it sounded like the cavalry had arrived.

SEVEN

Jones didn't make it all the way to the school before hitting police barricades. Not even trying to sweet-talk the officers who were frantically trying to direct traffic and deal with freaked-out parents, he parked his rental at a nearby business and ran the three blocks to the school.

He sought out the command center, not finding it hard to identify. There was a large RV-type vehicle with "Killeen PD Command Truck" painted on the side. There were several pockets of officers huddled around the back of the truck, looking at blueprints of the school as well as a group of lethal-looking men standing off to the side. Jones headed for them first.

"Fletch, Ghost. Good to see you."

Fletch stuck out his hand to shake Jones's. "You too, even if I wish it was under better circumstances."

Jones nodded at Ghost and shook his hand too, getting down to business. "What do we know?"

"Not much," Ghost told him grimly. "Apparently a lone shooter entered the front door around thirteen-forty. He didn't say anything, but started shooting from two hand guns."

"Casualties?" Jones asked.

"Three that we know of at this point. They were just inside the building and were the first shot. Thank God the school staff had been trained what to do in an active-shooter situation. Most of the classrooms have been evacuated. The teachers got the kids out the windows on the first floor. It might not have been the best decision, but I can't blame them. It's instinct to try to get out of the building where you know someone is shooting."

Jones nodded in relief. "Good. Shooter is still inside?"

"Yes," an unknown man answered that time. He'd walked up to their group as Ghost finished updating Jones with what he knew.

Jones looked at the officer and saw the tag on his uniform read "May." He held out his hand.

"Captain May, I'm Jones. I think you might've heard from my friend, Tex."

The other man nodded in agreement and shook his hand. "Yes. You're experienced in hostage negotiation?"

"Experienced as one can be when dealing with desperate people, I suppose. I just spent the last week down in Austin at a training seminar learning new techniques as well."

"Good. We've tapped into the surveillance cameras and it looks like the shooter is holed up in the gym. He's got two hostages. A first-grade teacher and a gym teacher. Miss O'Brien and Mr. Santoro seem to be holding their own at the moment."

"Excellent, gym teachers are usually in shape and we could use Mr. Santoro's help if need be," Jones mused.

"Oh, Tony isn't the gym teacher, he teaches first grade," Captain May explained. At the look of chagrin on Jones's face, he hurried to reassure him. "Don't worry about it, he gets that all the time. But he's former military. I spoke with the principal and she said they did a background check on him and he was some sort of Special Forces, but his records don't indicate what kind."

Jones and the other Deltas nodded. This was good. May didn't say what branch the man had been in, but ultimately it didn't matter. SEAL, Delta Force, Green Beret, British SAS or Australian Special Operations Command…any experience in the Special Forces would be appreciated and valuable in this situation. And they could use that right about now.

"What else do the cameras show?" Ghost demanded.

"The guy seems to be young. He's white, and a bad shot. He wounded a few people before everyone could get locked down."

"Kids?" Fletch interrupted, looking upset, and not like the in-control Delta Force soldier he was.

Jones spared a look at his friend, not sure why he sounded so stressed. Fletch was usually unflappable, but something about this situation had gotten to him. He didn't have time to reflect any more on it, however, as the captain answered.

"A few. But they played dead, as they were trained, thank God, and the guy kept on walking. Once he was out of sight, the kids helped each other up and came out the front of the school. They're being transported now, but none were injured badly."

"Are all the students out?" It was Jones who asked that time.

"We don't think so because the numbers aren't adding up," Captain May told them. "Of course we can't get a good count with all the chaos, but there's a teacher, Mrs. Brown, who says that she can't find *any* of the kids, and they were supposed to be in the gym. She hadn't picked them up before everything started. The principal says that Mr. Santoro's class also seems to be missing."

"He's the teacher who's in the gym with the shooter and the gym teacher?" Blade, one of the Delta Force soldiers, asked.

The captain nodded. "Miss O'Brien, yes. But the cameras in the gym only show the teachers and the shooter."

"Any chance I can get a look at those tapes?" Jones asked.

"Of course, we've got them pulled up inside the truck," Captain May agreed, turning to head toward the large vehicle without wasting any more time.

Jones, Ghost, and Fletch followed the officer, leaving the rest of the Deltas reviewing a set of blueprints of the building, and soon they were watching a live feed of the gym. All three men leaned in close. They couldn't hear what was being said, if anything, but they had a pretty good view of the large room.

"Is there audio?" Jones asked impatiently.

"Yeah, but it's not been switched on out here. We're just copying the feed. It's more complicated to copy it *and* get the audio. But inside there's audio capability," the captain explained quickly.

Jones nodded and continued to scope out the gym. There was a set of bleachers against one wall. There were about seven rows, all empty. On one end of the room there was a cluster of lockers. The floor of the gym had all sorts of equipment strewn around it, making entry, if necessary, more compli- cated. Tires, mats, flags, weights, and even a balance beam. The shooter was standing near the doors to the gym with a woman in his grasp. The gun he was holding was clearly visible, as was the tall bearded man about ten feet from them.

"As you can see, there's really no place to hide any kids…especially not two classes of them," May fretted.

Jones studied the layout of the gym and turned to Fletch. "You thinking what I'm thinking?"

"Yeah."

Jones turned to the police captain. He liked

Fletch's no-nonsense attitude. It almost felt as if he was back working on the teams again. Being on a Delta Force team was akin to working with brothers who had grown up together. They seemed to get each other without having to explain their thoughts. That was one of the reasons he enjoyed working with Joker. There was just something about the way a Special Forces operative's mind worked. They were in sync and it felt great.

"They're in the lockers," Jones told the captain, who blinked back at him in disbelief. "The teachers obviously had enough time to stash them there before the shooter arrived."

"How do you know that?" Captain May asked incredulously. "There's no way those kids would fit in there...would they?"

"There's nowhere else they *could* be," Jones said definitely. "They aren't under the bleachers, the shooter would've found them by now. The teachers could've hid under the bleachers themselves, but they didn't. And I figure they had to have had a reason not to do more to try to hide."

"God. *Damn*," the captain breathed.

"Yeah," Jones agreed. "The entire situation is a time bomb waiting to explode. All it'll take is one sneeze or cough from one of the kids, and their hiding spot will be compromised. We need to end this now."

"I'm making you our official hostage negotiator," Captain May declared. "The guy we usually use is about thirty minutes out, and we don't have that kind of time. Come on, you can use the microphone in the principal's office. It's connected to the speakers in every room in the building so announcements can be made. There's a two-way speaker in every room too, we'll turn it on in the gym so you can talk to him directly."

"Lead the way," Jones responded immediately, knowing as well as they all did that time was of the essence.

As they exited the command vehicle, Jones looked back at Fletch and Ghost. They nodded at him and turned to the rest of their team to bring them up to speed about the situation. Jones breathed out a relieved sigh. The Deltas would take care of security, and he could rely on them to be right where he needed them, *when* he needed them. Of that he had no doubt.

Following the police captain, Jones entered the principal's spacious office and settled himself behind the desk. Someone had called up the live feed of the gym on the computer already, and the microphone was there, ready to be used.

Jones nodded at the captain as he backed out of the room. He took a deep breath. This was what he did, what he'd trained for. Joker back in Virginia believed in him. His security teammates believed in him. And Mr. Santoro, Miss O'Brien, and two classes of kids were relying on him. He wouldn't fail.

He cleared his throat and pushed the transmit button on the microphone. He'd start out with the easy and expected line and go from there.

"My name is Jones. We have the building surrounded. Come out with your hands up."

EIGHT

Aimee winced as Bill's grasp tightened around her neck when he heard the voice over the loudspeaker. She kept her eyes on Tony, wanting to be ready for anything. She had no idea what he would be able to do, but she'd trust him with her life—*was* trusting him with her life at the moment.

"I want two million dollars and a helicopter," Bill shouted back at the unknown person on the other end of the speaker.

"You know that's not going to happen, man," the person responded, sounding almost amused. "I want to help you, but I can't if you make unreasonable demands. All I want is for you, Mr. Santoro, and Miss O'Brien to come out of this alive. Okay?"

"How does he know your names?" Bill hissed into Aimee's ear.

"I don't know," she managed to squeak out. "I'm guessing the principal told him we weren't outside and they assumed it was us in here." Aimee knew good and well there were cameras in each classroom, and the gym. She'd resented them when she'd first started, feeling as if she was being spied on, but had quickly lost interest in them. It wasn't as if the principal or anyone else was sitting around watching her teach, they had their own work to get done. Besides that, they really were a good tool when people had to observe the class, or in cases of emergencies...like this one.

"I guess we'll see how much they like you then," Bill mused before raising his voice to respond to the mystery man on the other end of the electronic device. "You don't give a shit about me, so don't pretend you do. You cops have no clue what life is really about. You sit in your fancy-ass cars, with your fancy-ass houses, with your fancy-ass wives, and look down on the rest of us who are struggling to get by. You're so clueless, you have no idea your wife is probably fucking the neighbor the second you leave to go to work."

"I'm not a cop," the voice said, seemingly not

ruffled in the least. "My name is Jones, and I work for an security company in Virginia."

Aimee was just as confused as Bill obviously was.

He muttered under his breath, "What the fuck?" before saying it louder. "What the fuck? What is someone from Virginia doing talking to me here in Texas?"

"I happened to be here on vacation," Jones replied nonchalantly.

"Lucky me," Bill said under his breath again. Then louder, he mocked, "Well, Jones, if that's even your name, your wife is probably having a grand old time fucking your best friend back home on the beach while you're here in this shithole of a town."

Aimee had no idea what protocol was in these kinds of situations, but the man who'd called himself Jones seemed to have no sense of urgency in his voice. It was as if he was chatting Bill up at a party or something. She looked over at Tony. He was standing stock still now, but she'd noticed he'd moved about a foot closer to where Bill was standing with her in his tight grasp.

Tony's shoulder was still bleeding, if the enlarging stain on his shirt was any indication. Amazingly though, he acted as if he didn't even realize he was hurt. He wasn't holding on to his arm, and didn't even seem to be favoring it. Aimee had no idea how badly he was hurt, but surely it had to be superficial, because she figured otherwise he'd be swaying, or swearing, or something.

One thing she *did* know was that she'd never forget the way Tony looked right this moment. It was inappropriate as hell, but she figured God would cut her some slack if she died right now, because Tony was…glorious.

His hands were fisted at his sides, as if he was holding himself back by a mere thread. His eyes were narrowed, and focused on Bill and her. She couldn't see his jaw under the beard, but she imagined he was probably clenching his teeth in aggravation. Amazingly, his hair was still up in a messy bun at the back of his neck, but she could see some strands of hair hanging loose around his face. He looked like an avenging angel. *Her* avenging angel.

But it was Tony's eyes that fascinated her the most. He was standing about nine feet away from them at this point, but she didn't think she was imagining the emotion she saw in his glittering brown eyes.

When he was looking at Bill, she could see determination and frustration in his eyes, but when he turned his gaze to her, she could see affection and reassurance in them. It was crazy, she'd tell anyone who tried to explain they could see emotions in someone's eyes that they were being silly, but at that moment she would've bet everything she owned that she was right.

It gave her hope.

It gave her confidence.

It gave her the ability to stay calm, even as Bill's arm tightened around her neck painfully.

She wanted that kiss from Tony. She wanted more than that, but she'd start with a kiss. Aimee knew she just had to be patient.

She wasn't dumb. At any time, Bill could decide he was done with the back and forth and shoot her and Tony before any help could get to them, but she wasn't going to call it quits quite yet. She wasn't a quitter. She was going to fight for her life, and Tony's, and the lives of the thirty-six children hiding across the room.

"Actually, Jones *is* my name." the disembodied voice returned. "And yeah, I've been made fun of my entire life because of it. Having a last name as my first has been a pain in my ass, but my mama gave it to me, and I love that woman with everything in me. She was a single parent and raised me in Compton. You've heard of Compton, right, Bill? Every day I walked home from school past drug dealers and prostitutes. I knew how to inject meth and snort cocaine by the time I was nine. So yeah, I have some idea of what it's like to struggle to get by."

"But here you are, on the right side of the law. Aren't you just the poster child for getting out of your piss poor situation?" Bill retorted, not willing to give an inch.

"I was arrested three times before I was eighteen," Jones continued, as if Bill wasn't insulting him with every breath, his voice echoing throughout the vast room. "The last time I did a stint in juvie because I hit a cop. I was forced to join the Army after that, and it was the best thing I ever did. I hated the drill sergeants yelling at me all the time, but I learned that sometimes it's better to work as a team, to be quiet and act with professionalism. Life is a struggle, Bill. Every single damn day. I'm not married, but if I was, I wouldn't stay with a woman who opened her legs for my neighbor or best friend. I deserve more than that. You do too. You deserve a woman who loves you for who you are, not for how much money you have or what you do for a living."

Aimee noticed two things at the same time.

Something this Jones guy had said resonated with Tony. He suddenly lost some of his focus on her and Bill and his eyes started to subtly wander the room, as if he was looking for something. Secondly, Jones's words seemed to be having an effect on Bill as well. His arm loosened a fraction, not enough for her to move away from him, or even break away, but enough that it took the pressure off her windpipe, allowing her to breathe a little easier.

She took deep breaths, filling her lungs with fresh air, readying herself for when he'd tighten against her again.

"I won't lie to you, Bill," Jones's disembodied voice went on. "You're in trouble here. We both know that, and I'm not gonna feed you a line about giving up and walking out of there a free man. But what's happened doesn't mean the end of your life. Yeah, you'll do some time, but it won't be forever. You're young...what...twenty-three?"

"Two," Bill answered absently.

"Twenty-two then. I don't know what happened today to make you think this was the best solution, but—"

"You ever been ignored, Jones?" Bill interrupted. "Ignored so much in your life that no matter what you do, no one sees you?"

"Yeah, I have."

"Bullshit!" Bill roared, scaring the shit out of Aimee and making her jump in his arms. "I'm not talking about a woman choosing your buddy to suck his cock in the back hallway of a seedy bar, I'm talking about every day of your life, by every single person you've ever met."

"Then, no. I haven't been ignored like that," Jones said calmly.

"Right, then you have no idea what it's like to walk down the street and not have one person look you in the eyes. To bring your items to the check-out line and have the lady behind the register not look up at you once. To be at a high-school dance and stand against the wall the entire time as if you're not even there. I'm invisible, man. I've *always* been invisible."

"That's tough, Bill," Jones commiserated. "Is that why you did it? So you'd be seen?"

"Damn right. I can't be ignored now," Bill said, the heat back in his voice. "Good job, Tina. You jumped so high in your cheerleading routine," he singsonged, as if remembering the voice of someone else. "Wow, Tina, that cake you baked came out perfect. Way to go, Tina, you got all A's this quarter. Tina, Tina, Tina. It was always fucking

Tina. I brought home all A's for an entire year, and I didn't get one word of recognition. So I tried failing everything, but all I got was an eye-roll. I could've dropped out and that bitch wouldn't have even noticed. Until you've been where I am, you can't understand."

"So you did something no one could ignore. Good job, Bill," Jones said dryly. "You've got all the recognition you can handle and more."

"Yeah, damn straight," Bill agreed.

"So what now?" Jones pushed. "You've got two hostages and the attention you've always wanted. How do we get out of this?"

Bill raised the barrel of the pistol to Aimee's head. "I'm *not* going to jail. I'll be ignored there too...except when assholes want to make me their fuck toy. This ends here. I need to make sure I won't be ignored even when I'm dead. Everyone's gonna remember my name. William Walter Waters. I'm gonna be famous."

Aimee refused to close her eyes. If she was going to die, the last thing she wanted to see was Tony's face, not the backside of her eyelids. And she *was* going to die. She could feel the determination in Bill's hold on her. The barrel of the gun pressed into her temple hard enough that she knew it was going to leave a mark. She chuckled morosely to herself; a bullet would leave much more of a mark, it was silly to even be thinking about what she'd look like when Bill pulled the trigger, but she couldn't help it.

She vaguely heard Jones's voice in the background, but had no idea what he was saying. Aimee kept her eyes on Tony. She had no idea if she had only seconds to live, but if he gave her any indication of something she could do to stay alive, she'd see it and act.

She wanted to live, dammit.

She *wanted* it.

With every fiber of her being.

Bill leaned down and whispered in her ear, his voice blowing her hair in a way that would've been seductive if it was a different time, a different place, and a different person.

"My apologies to Billy the Kid and Emilio Estevez for screwing up their line...but you're gonna make me famous, Miss O'Brien."

NINE

Jones kept talking, trying to get Bill to concentrate on him rather than on whatever asinine plan he had in mind. He knew without a doubt that the man would kill both hostages if he could. For a kid who'd been ignored his entire life, and compared to an over-performing sister, getting recognition by being a killer seemed to be a perfect solution to finally get people to pay attention to him.

Bill wasn't a terrorist. He had no agenda, other than to get people to see him. And he'd certainly succeeded in that. He was being seen all right.

Jones had tried to let Mr. Santoro, Tony, know that he was Delta, but had no idea if his subtle clue had worked. Using "quiet" and "professionalism" was a direct reference to something Delta soldiers said many times, no matter where they were stationed or trained. It was an unofficial motto that had been passed down through the years. Jones had no idea what branch of Special Forces Tony had been, but he hoped he'd recognize the reference regardless.

Deltas were known as quiet professionals because they were top-secret and did what they had to do without anyone knowing about it. The world knew about Navy SEALs and what they did, but Deltas were the great unknown. People knew they existed, but every single mission was top secret and even knowing who was on the teams was kept quiet.

Knowing Bill was done talking to him, that nothing he was saying was getting through to the young man, Jones hoped like hell the Deltas were ready. This was about to be over in a very bloody way and he'd done all he could to make sure the elite Army team had enough time to get into place.

Looking at the video in front of him, all Jones could do was watch, and wait, for the shit to hit the fan.

Aimee had been concentrating so hard on watching Tony's eyes, seeing the emotions play out in them, that she almost missed his signal. Bill was still whispering in her ear, but she'd tuned him out. It was if she was in a long tunnel, and the only thing she could see was Tony at the end of it. Sounds were muted, and she felt as if she was watching the scene from the rafters lining the gym ceiling instead of being in the middle of it.

Tony's eyes shifted. He looked down, then back up at her. He did it again, this time lowering his chin at the same time he dropped his eyes. Aimee wanted to believe it was a signal, but she couldn't be sure. Unfortunately, she had no time to wait around and try to decide if what she was seeing was really a signal to drop to the floor or not.

It'd be tricky, she was currently being held up by Bill's arm around her throat, but she'd do it. Anything was better than her brains being splattered across the gym floor. And if she was wrong, misinterpreting Tony's actions—it was possible it was just a tick or something—maybe her actions would force Bill, Tony, the cops outside, Jones...*someone* to do something.

Bill was mid-sentence, saying something about making history, when Aimee let herself go limp in his arms. His hold around her neck tightened painfully, completely blocking her air for a split-second.

Aimee wasn't a big woman, but she was muscular. Her weight, and the surprise of her dropping, made Bill lose his grip on her and her knees crashed into the hard wooden floor of the gym.

What seemed like simultaneously, shots rang out and echoed across the gym. Aimee whimpered in fright, waiting for the pain of a bullet to hit her, sure Bill had pulled the trigger as he'd been threatening. Her eyes involuntarily squeezed closed, shutting out everything around her.

Sound was muted, she heard noises, but wasn't sure exactly what she was hearing. Grunts, moans, and shouts…but she stayed huddled on the ground in a small ball, trying to make herself as inconspicuous as possible.

Aimee felt herself being embraced. She wasn't moved, wasn't shifted in any way. Arms and warmth surrounded her as she shook in delayed reaction to everything that had happened. She didn't dare open her eyes, too scared of what she'd see. It was cowardly of her, but she'd reached the end of her rope. All thoughts of dying as she looked into Tony's eyes were long gone.

Slowly, her senses returned and she heard words being murmured in her ear, over and over.

"I got you. It's okay, I got you, Aimee. You're okay. You're safe. We're all right. I got you."

I got you.

She knew in an instant it was Tony crooning to her. She didn't move, but opened her eyes into slits, taking that first step into dealing with the aftermath of what had happened.

She couldn't distinguish much because of her position on the floor, but she saw several pairs of boots standing near them, and heard lots of talking all at once. The wooden planks of the gym floor surrounding her were splattered with red paint... no, not paint.

Feeling vulnerable, and finally realizing the delayed need to protect herself, she whipped her head around to look for Bill.

He was lying behind her, on his back, arms outstretched, gun still clasped in his hand. His eyes were open and staring up at the rafters. There was a small red stain slowly spreading on his shirt, and a larger puddle oozing out from under him.

Aimee didn't even flinch. She'd never wished death on anyone, no matter how bad they were, but at that moment she was more than happy that it was Bill lying on the floor dead, rather than her or Tony or any of the children.

"I got you, Aimee." Tony repeated the words and Aimee felt them soak into her soul. She knew she'd never forget this moment, or his words. They were just what she needed to calm her, to make her able to deal with the situation.

"The kids, we have to get them out," she stated resolutely, trying to stand up.

Tony moved out of her way enough to let her stand, but he was right there next to her, his arms still around her, holding her tightly when she stood upright.

"They're in the lockers, right?" a voice to their left asked.

Aimee turned her head, not willing to pull herself out of Tony's arms yet. She saw a tall man, obviously military, even though he was in jeans and a black T-shirt. He had the kind of conceited, "I can take care of everything" look about him. His arms were covered in tattoos and he had blue eyes.

"Yeah, it was the only place we could think of to hide them," she answered affirmatively.

"I had nothing to do with that decision," Tony told the soldier. "It was all Aimee."

For a second she thought Tony was throwing

her under the proverbial bus with his words, but realized almost at the same time, that he was giving her credit for the decision, rather than having the man standing next to them think it was his doing.

"Good job, ma'am. How many kids?"

"Thirty-six," Aimee answered. She knew she should probably go and help keep the students calm, but she didn't have it in her at the moment. Realizing something, she blurted out, "Take them through one of the locker-rooms so they don't have to see him." She motioned toward Bill's bleeding body. "They've been through enough."

"Of course." With that, the man jogged around the obstacle course equipment Aimee had set up what seemed like years ago.

"You okay?" Tony asked in a low voice next to her.

Aimee looked up at him for the first time since the bullets had started flying. Surprised to see such a tender, concerned look on his face, she could only nod.

"God, you were awesome. I'm probably not supposed to say that, but it's true." Tony looked around for a moment, then his eyes came back to hers. "We don't have a lot of time before the cops descend, but in a nutshell, Jones is Special Forces, or former Special Forces or something. I knew by something he said that there'd be others nearby just waiting for the perfect time to act. I didn't know if you'd understand me or not, but since you hadn't taken your eyes off of me the entire time, I'd hoped."

"I saw," Aimee said simply.

Tony nodded. "It wasn't the best plan, but it was all we had. I knew if we could give the guys a shot at Bill, they'd take it. Hell, they'd probably take it even if you hadn't moved, but *I* didn't want to take that chance."

"Thank you."

"For what?"

"For being here. For helping me with the kids. For being a voice of reason." Aimee stroked his bloody arm. "Thank you for being the man you are. I wouldn't have been able to stay calm if you weren't here with me."

"Bull," Tony countered immediately. "You're a professional down to your bones. You would've done the exact same thing if I wasn't here."

"But I'm glad you were," Aimee whispered.

Before Tony could respond, they were interrupted by a large man in a police uniform.

"Miss O'Brien? Mr. Santoro? I'm Captain May.

I'm certainly glad to see you alive and well. EMS will be here in a moment to take a look at that arm, but I'm going to need both your statements about what happened here today."

Aimee nodded, and Tony did the same. He held out his hand to the captain and they shook hands. "Thanks for getting here so quickly."

They all turned upon hearing the commotion on the other side of the gym. The kids were being let out of the lockers two by two. They looked scared and shaken up, but they were alive. It was all that mattered.

One of the children, a first-grader named Bridget, saw her favorite teachers from across the gym and took off around the officers and military guys trying to herd them toward the locker rooms. She made a beeline for Aimee and Tony.

"Miss O'Brien! Mr. Santoro!" she wailed as she ran.

"Shit," Aimee murmured under her breath, worried about Bridget seeing the bloody mess nearby.

"Get her," Tony ordered. "I'll cover you."

Aimee stepped toward Bridget and opened her arms. The little girl ran right into them without looking away. Aimee folded her arms around the small child and turned so the girl's back was facing Bill. She held on tight, not loosening her hold for a moment when she felt Bridget's tiny body shaking and trembling with the force of her tears and fright.

"You're okay, Bridget. Everything's fine."

"I was so s-s-scared," she blubbered.

"But you did good. I didn't hear one peep from anyone. That was amazing," Aimee praised.

"Tommy held me the whole time," Bridget said, finally picking her head up off of her gym teacher's belly and looking up. "He was scared too, but we didn't make any noise."

"Good girl," Tony soothed. "No wonder you get all A's in my class. You're super smart."

Her teacher's praise obviously went a long way toward making the dark-haired girl feel better.

"Go on now, you need to get outside with the others. I know your daddy will be worried about you. He'll want to see for himself that you're all right," Tony told her, obviously knowing his students well. Bridget's mom had never been in her life and her dad was a soldier raising his small daughter by himself. He'd be beside himself worrying about her, as would all the parents.

"Okay. See you tomorrow!"

Tony and Aimee watched as one of the officers

sent to retrieve the runaway child escorted her to the locker room, careful to block her view of the violence nearby. Aimee felt Tony step next to her, getting into her personal space.

"You need to change," he told Aimee in a weird voice.

"What?"

But he didn't repeat himself, merely worked on unbuttoning his dress shirt to give to her. "It's not exactly clean, but I'm guessing you might prefer my blood on you, over his. I'll have to take this off anyway so the medics can get to my arm."

Aimee watched in confusion, and with some awe, as Tony stripped off his shirt and held it out to her. It took her a moment to realize why he was giving her his shirt, and she turned her head to try to see behind her back.

Tony took her chin in his hand and kept her from seeing the blood that had splattered onto her when Bill was shot. "I'll block the view of the others. Just take it off and drop it. You'll be covered up in a jiffy."

Aimee nodded, not comfortable at all in stripping off her T-shirt in front of all the men and women wandering around the gym, but she wanted

Bill's blood off of her more than she wanted privacy.

"Don't pull it over your head," Tony ordered suddenly. "Pull your arms out and ease it off that way, so the outside of it doesn't touch your skin. I'll use the inside of it to get as much blood out of your hair as I can. There isn't much."

Aimee shivered, thankful for his direction. She would've whipped the shirt off as fast as she could if he hadn't warned her, turning it inside out and getting Bill's blood all over her skin in the process. She shuddered, thinking about that as she did as Tony suggested. She was standing in front of him in nothing but a white sports bra before she even thought about what she was doing.

Tony's nostrils flared and his eyes glittered, letting Aimee know he liked what he was seeing. But he didn't act on it and in no way showed her any disrespect. He simply took his shirt and wrapped it around her back and waited until she put her arms through. He pulled it closed around her and started doing up the buttons.

"I'm sorry about not thinking about this earlier," he told her. "I wish I had a clean one to give you."

"It's okay," Aimee told him honestly, taking a

deep breath and smelling his soap on the shirt. It felt as if they were still on the ground and he had his hands around her, all while he whispered, "I got you." She clutched her hands around her belly tightly, holding onto herself.

Her eyes roamed the masculine chest in front of her. He was wearing a tight white undershirt, which molded to his pecs and biceps as if painted on. She could see his pulse beating at his throat and felt his breath on her cheeks.

"Thank you."

"You're welcome."

"You should probably get that arm looked at."

Tony nodded. "Yeah, in a minute, after I help you with your hair."

Aimee nodded and held still as he used her shirt, now inside out, to wipe down her hair. She tried not to think about how awesome a shower would feel, knowing it would be quite a while before that fantasy could become reality.

He finished, dropping the shirt on the floor as if he couldn't bear to hold it any longer and silence settled between them. She turned to face him, looking up into his face. Aimee could almost feel the electricity arcing between them.

"About that date," Aimee said breathlessly.

"Yeah?"

"If you're not busy later tonight, after we get through whatever it is that we need to get through, I wouldn't mind some company."

Tony breathed out a sigh of relief. "Good. Because I was going to show up at your place whether we had a date or not. I think I need to make sure you're really all right."

"You want to babysit me?"

"No. I'm saying this badly," Tony admitted. "I don't want to be alone. Today brought up way too many memories for me. If I go back to my place, I'll relive every second of what happened and there's no way I'll be able to sleep and not have nightmares. I'd like to hang out with you. Eat. Watch a movie. Talk. Whatever."

"I'd like that too. I don't want to be alone either."

"Then I'll see you later?"

Aimee nodded then boldly leaned forward and rested her forehead on Tony's chest and felt his arms wrap around her waist. They stood like that for a minute or two before a paramedic reluctantly interrupted them.

"Mr. Santoro? I think you'd better let me get a look at that arm."

Aimee backed up and looked up at the man who had changed her life forever. It seemed like she'd always known him. They'd lived a lifetime in the last thirty minutes. Dating games didn't seem to matter so much anymore. She wanted this man in her life. She wanted *him*.

He leaned down and kissed her forehead in a tender gesture that made her heart beat faster in her chest. "Take care of yourself. I'll see you later."

"Miss O'Brien? We'd like to take your statement now, if that's okay," an officer from the Killeen Police Department told her in a respectful voice. She took a deep breath, knowing she'd be busy the rest of the day with law enforcement and most likely the press as well. She'd have to talk to the principal, as well as reassure the kids she came across that everything was fine.

Suddenly Aimee had so many questions. Were all the students okay? Was anyone killed? She wanted to see all of the kids. She knew every single one, since they all rotated in and out of her gym. Was Annie all right? Aimee would hate if her sunny disposition was dampened in any way. What about the others in the gym with them? Had they heard everything Bill and Jones had said back and forth? Did they understand it? Would they be scarred for life? She had so many questions and no answers.

Thinking about the man who called himself Jones made her want to thank him in person. She hadn't thought much about negotiation techniques before today, but Jones had made it sound easy. He'd been calm and cool and had even managed to send a secret message to Tony. It was amazing and she wanted to see him face-to-face and show him her appreciation.

Aimee's mind spun. She had so many things she wanted to do, but didn't know what to do first.

"If you'll follow me, we'll go out into the command vehicle where it's a bit calmer than in here. We'll get this out of the way and I'll see if I can't answer some of the questions I can see swirling around in your brain. Okay?" the officer informed her, holding out his hand as if to show her the way.

"Yeah, thanks. It's all catching up to me and I do have so many things I want to know."

"Come on, the sooner we get this done, the sooner you can get home to a shower and a nice soft bed."

Aimee nodded in agreement and followed the officer out of the gym.

TEN

Aimee sat on her couch and breathed a sigh of relief. It was seven at night, and the last five hours had been excruciatingly long. First, she'd been drilled by the officer for an hour about what had happened. He wanted to know every word she could remember, everything she and Tony had done, what she'd heard, even what she *thought* about the entire situation.

After the interrogation...err...interview was over, she'd asked to speak with Jones, the man whose voice she knew, but whose face she wouldn't recognize if she passed him on the street. The officer had nodded and within twenty minutes, the door to the RV opened and a man strode in who was most obviously military, law enforcement, or some other kind of badass.

He was tall and stern looking, but it was the look of compassion and relief in his eyes that had struck her the most. He was a person in a shitty situation, just like she'd been.

Standing up to shake his hand, she'd been surprised when he engulfed her small frame in a bear hug.

"God *damn* is it good to meet you," he told her fervently.

Aimee giggled. "I think that's my line."

"I've been doing this a while now, but I have to say you and Mr. Santoro were the most levelheaded hostages I've had the pleasure of witnessing."

"Maybe outwardly," Aimee mumbled against his chest, as he hadn't let go of her yet.

At her comment, he'd pulled away slightly and looked down at her. "Outwardly is all that matters. I don't care if you were screaming like a newborn baby on the inside, it's your actions that count when push comes to shove. You hid the kids, didn't panic, and provided a distraction just when it was needed."

"I don't remember what you said there at the end," Aimee admitted. "I have no idea what *Bill* was even saying. All I could do was watch Tony and wait for some sort of signal from him."

"It doesn't matter what was said. All that matters is that you did what needed to be done."

"Did he really come into an elementary school shooting because he didn't feel like people were paying attention to him?" Aimee asked.

Jones pulled back all the way and put his hands on her shoulders. His voice got serious. "Apparently. But honestly, it doesn't really matter what the motive was. People who want to kill will find a way. They'll use guns, bombs, knives, baseball bats, tire irons…whatever it takes. There's *always* a motivation. It could be they stubbed their toe that morning. Maybe they felt ignored growing up, like Bill. Abuse, neglect, or it could be the way they're raised. Politics, religion and ideological beliefs are always there as ready excuses as well. It doesn't matter. We can't control it, and I honestly don't believe we can stop it. The only thing we *can* do is be ready for it. To act when it does happen. Protect ourselves and those around us as best we can. And I have to say, Aimee O'Brien, you did good."

"Thanks," Aimee whispered, overwhelmed with his words. Needing to change the subject, as it was way too intense for her. "Are you really on vacation?"

Jones laughed and dropped his hands from her shoulders, putting them in his pockets and stepping away from her. "Sort of. I do work with and security company in Virginia. My boss was A Navy SEAL and in law enforcement. We work with all sorts of situations like the one today. I was in Austin this past week for a hostage negotiation conference."

"Well, *that* was good timing," Aimee said in awe.

"Agreed. I know some guys up here in Killeen who work for the Army. I just happened to be in the right place at the right time."

"Thank God," Aimee drawled.

"Yup. You gonna be all right?" Jones asked.

"Yes," Aimee declared immediately. "No way am I gonna let some asshole ruin my life."

"Good for you. If you're ever in Virginia, I'll consider it extremely rude if you don't look me up to say hello."

Aimee laughed. "I hadn't planned on any vacations to the mountains in the near future, but I might just have to make the effort now."

Jones held out his hand. Aimee took it and they sealed the deal. "You're good people, Aimee."

"Back at'cha, Jones."

They'd said their goodbyes and Aimee's next job was dealing with the media. Even though the shootout had been over fairly quickly and there hadn't been that many casualties, the news stations were rabid over the incident. There were trucks and cars parked everywhere and reporters were roving the grounds of the school with their faithful camera operators following them closely.

Knowing it needed to be done, Aimee had asked Captain May to set up a couple of interviews, just to get them over with. She didn't have to do it, the school board president or someone else on the board could handle it, but since she was directly involved, it seemed like the right thing to do. She wasn't naïve enough to believe it would be the end of it, but for once in her life she hoped some other newsworthy event would happen soon to trump this one so everyone, especially the students, could be left alone to heal.

Next, she'd sought out the groups of students who hadn't been picked up yet. They'd all been herded into the cafeteria, which was on the other side of the school from the gym. She'd cuddled and talked about what had happened with the kids, listening when they wanted to talk, and simply hugging the ones who needed the one-on-one human contact.

Principal Allen had also wanted information on what had happened in the gym. Aimee had told the story so many times she wanted to scream, but she simply retold it again and again and again, to whoever wanted to hear it, gritted her teeth and continued on.

It'd been an extremely emotionally draining day and now she was finally home. It was dark outside and slightly chilly…just how she felt inside. Aimee was starving, but didn't have the energy to get up and make something to eat. It'd been a long time since the sandwich and chips she'd eaten with Tony at lunch, the fuel from the calories long gone.

She'd showered and changed as soon as she'd arrived home. Tony's shirt was bloody, dirty, and needed to be washed. It was silly to worry about cleaning it, because he'd probably just chuck it, there was a hole in the sleeve after all, but Aimee made the decision that if he didn't want it, she'd keep it to sleep in…just to remember how good it felt when he'd taken care of her by taking it off and giving it to her.

I got you.

His words still rang in her head. She was a

former soldier, a fully competent woman who could take care of herself, and *had* taken care of herself for her entire adult life. She'd bought her own house, mowed her own lawn, invested her money without help from anyone else, but those three words wouldn't leave her brain.

The ding-dong of the doorbell pealed through the small house, jolting Aimee out of her musings. She sighed. She couldn't deal with anything else. Not one more reporter, not one more question from the police, not one more surprise.

She ignored it and closed her eyes, hoping whoever it was would go away if she didn't answer the door.

The bell rang again.

Sighing deeply, and pulling up her big-girl panties, Aimee rose from the couch and headed for the door. She looked through the peephole, and was pleasantly surprised to see Tony on the other side. He'd *said* he wanted to come over, but Aimee had assumed he was as tired as she was. He had probably gone through all the same things she had today after the shootout.

She unlocked the door and swung it open, welcoming the one man who would truly understand what she was feeling at that moment, since he'd been right there alongside her when her world had almost ended.

"Hi!"

"Hi. I wasn't sure if you still wanted me to come over, but I took the chance."

"Of course I did. I'm glad you're here. Come in," Aimee told him, holding the door open wider.

Tony held up some white paper bags. "I brought food."

"Oh my God, you're my hero. Get in here!" Aimee ordered, reaching out and grabbing the front of his shirt and pulling him into her entryway.

He laughed, and followed her willingly.

"You look...different," Aimee told him, blushing for some reason. She hadn't realized it until she'd grabbed the front of his shirt, but he was wearing jeans and a T-shirt. Other than the one time at the carnival at the school, she'd never seen him in anything other than his dress shirts, a tie, and a pair of slacks. He looked more...rugged, approachable, down-to-earth, relaxed...a hundred other adjectives came to mind.

Tony shrugged. "Believe it or not, I don't wear a tie on my time off."

Aimee laughed, as he'd expected her to. "I

know, I'm sorry. It's just different. Not bad different. Just different. What did you bring to eat?"

"I stopped by my favorite hole-in-the-wall Mexican place. Loads of chips and salsa, and tacos. I didn't want to get too crazy because I wasn't sure what you liked or if you'd already eaten."

"I hope you brought a lot. I could eat a dozen tacos right about now. Do you mind eating on the couch? It's really comfortable and I don't care if we spill anything on it."

"Couch sounds wonderful," Tony told her. "Can I grab the drinks?"

"I'll get them, thanks though. Go through there and get settled, I'll be there in a bit. Water okay?"

"Perfect."

By the time Aimee got back into her small living room, Tony had opened two containers of salsa, torn open one of the bags to make a bowl of sorts for the chips, and had put what looked at first glance like twenty wrapped tacos in a row on the coffee table.

The smell emanating from the feast made her mouth water. The two made small talk as they consumed the meal, but otherwise didn't go out of their way to communicate, too engrossed in the delicious food filling their bellies.

Finally, when there were only two tacos left and the remnants of chips and salsa, Aimee flopped back on the couch and groaned.

"Oh my God, I couldn't eat another bite."

"Are you quoting Monty Python?" Tony teased.

Smiling, Aimee told him, "No, but if I ate even a single mint I *would* explode."

They shared a laugh and Tony drank the rest of the water out of his bottle and placed it on the table in front of him. He also sat back, obviously replete and satisfied now that he'd eaten.

"Thank you for not only bringing dinner, but for coming over."

"I wasn't sure you still wanted me to show up." Tony repeated what he'd told her at the door.

"I wanted you to show up," Aimee reassured him firmly. "I'm so tired, I think I could fall asleep standing up, but I know the second I close my eyes, I'll most likely relive everything that happened today."

Tony didn't move, but put his arm on the back of the couch and turned his head to her. "If it helps, I feel exactly the same way. Any chance you'd let me hold you for a bit?"

Without thinking about it, knowing she wanted to be in his arms again more than she wanted her next breath, Aimee scooted over on the cushions and curled into his chest. She brought both feet up and braced them on the edge of the couch and snaked one arm behind his back, the other over his stomach. She immediately felt his arm, which had been on the back of the couch, come down around her shoulders.

"How's the arm? I should've asked that before I attacked the food," Aimee murmured, shifting into him, getting more comfortable. She felt his words reverberate against the top of her head when he answered.

"Good. The bullet just grazed me. Bled like a stuck pig, but it wasn't life threatening at all."

"I'm glad. You were lucky."

"*We* were lucky," he returned.

They sat in silence for a while, enjoying the feel of the human contact.

"I hope you don't mind me asking," Aimee said gently, "but are you *really* okay after today? It's obvious you were affected by the gunshots…more than the average person."

Aimee felt Tony sigh under her. She didn't dare look up at him. She knew that sometimes it was easier to talk about tough things when you didn't have to look someone in the eye.

"I can't talk about most of it, but yeah, I get reminded of my time on the teams almost every day. A student drops a book on the floor, a car backfires, someone smacks their hand on a desk…it's not one thing that I remember…it's more a collection of all the missions I've been on. It seemed like it would be a lot easier to get past it all when I was talking about getting out, huddled in a bombed-out building in the middle of some godforsaken village overseas than it's been in reality."

"You've seen a lot."

"I've seen a lot," Tony confirmed in a tortured voice.

"Thank you for your service," Aimee told him, sitting up and looking at him, wanting him to see her sincerity. "I know I've said it before, probably too much, but I mean it. I told you that I was never deployed when I was in, but that doesn't mean that I don't get it. I appreciate you and all of your comrades more than I can say. I know I'll remember today and what those shots sounded like for the rest of my life, but it's different for me because the outcome was for the most part, positive."

"I'm here if you ever need to talk about it," Tony told her immediately.

"Thanks. I'm sure I'll need to. I appreciate that more than you'll know," Aimee sighed, snuggling back into his side.

"Do you think you can sleep?"

"Maybe."

"Do you want me to go?"

"No! You said you didn't want to be alone either. Are you comfortable? We'll sleep like this. If that's all right?"

"Yeah."

Aimee closed her eyes, expecting to see the crazy look in Bill's eyes as he pointed his guns in their direction, but instead all she saw were *Tony's* eyes. She inhaled deeply, pulling his unique scent into her lungs, and relaxed farther into him.

"You smell delicious," she murmured sleepily.

"Eau de soap," Tony teased.

"It's soap, but it's also you," Aimee insisted.

He didn't respond, but she felt his arm tighten around her back and his other hand come up to rest on her arm lying on his belly.

She didn't remember falling asleep and didn't dream at all.

ELEVEN

It took Aimee a moment to remember what had happened when she woke up a few hours later. Somehow, after she'd fallen asleep, Tony had shifted them so they were both lying down on her couch. His head was resting on the end of the sofa and he was holding her secure in his arms. Their legs were tangled together and her back was resting against the couch.

She never felt more comfortable in all her life. Aimee fit against Tony perfectly. Lifting her head, she gazed at Tony's face without feeling self-conscious about it because he had no idea she was watching him. His mouth was open as he slightly snored and she could see his pupils moving back and forth under his lids. His hair was strewn about his shoulders in disarray, making him seem even sexier.

Aimee lifted her hand and did what she'd been dreaming about for months. She put her palm on his cheek and felt his beard against her hand. She wasn't sure what she expected, but the hair was soft and Aimee felt a shiver run through her. Her dirty mind immediately wondered what it would feel like against her inner thighs, or her stomach, or even against her lips.

She eyed his lips, curious as to how it would feel to kiss someone with a beard. Her fingers unconsciously stroked against his cheek, learning the contours of his face while enjoying the feel of his facial hair on her skin.

"What time is it?"

Aimee jolted, taken by surprise at Tony's soft words. She immediately removed her hand from his face, embarrassed she'd been caught touching him without his permission. His arm moved and he put his palm over her hand, pressing it back against his cheek, nuzzling into her touch.

"I'm not sure," Aimee told him, answering his question. "It's still dark outside."

"You okay?"

Loving that one of his first thoughts was to ask

how she was doing, Aimee said, "Surprisingly, yeah. You?"

"I'm good. I can't remember the last time I've been this comfortable."

"When I bought the couch I made sure I tested it by lying on it before deciding."

"It's not the sofa that's making me comfortable," Tony told her, chuckling a little.

Aimee didn't say anything for a moment, understanding what he meant but slightly embarrassed by it nonetheless. Finally she said, "I have to say that you're the best pillow I've ever had."

He chuckled louder now and Aimee felt his chest move under hers. "You like the feel of my beard?"

Tony moved his head a little, rubbing against her hand, and Aimee shivered. "I've never felt one like yours before. I mean, I've felt a five o'clock shadow, but not like yours. Not many men can pull it off like you can. I like it."

"Good." He was quiet for a moment, then said, "I want to kiss you. Not as part of a bet, but because we both want it."

"Yes, please," Aimee sighed, knowing somehow that her life was about to change…for the better.

Tony didn't immediately lunge at her or otherwise attack her. He stared up at her in the darkness of the room. A light in the kitchen was still on, so they could see each other. He brought one hand up to her hair and smoothed it over her head, caressing her back as he went. His hand stopped at her lower back and pressed her into him.

Licking her lips, Aimee could feel his heart beating strongly under her. She waited with bated breath for him to make a move. Finally, he put his free hand under her chin, tilting her head up toward him. His head slowly came toward her own, stretching out the moment until Aimee thought she was going to scream, "Get on with it already!"

Aimee kept her eyes open until the second his lips touched hers. She inhaled deeply, smelling the delicious scent that was uniquely his, and surrendered herself to Tony.

Their first kiss was chaste and sweet, a mere touching of lips together. Aimee felt him smile before his lips were covering hers again. He put gentle pressure on her chin, moving it to the side to give him more room. He nipped and sucked, then finally she felt his tongue ease inside her mouth.

Meeting it with her own, she dueled with him, learning the taste and feel of his mouth. What had started out as a sweet get-to-know-you kiss, quickly spiraled into something more elemental and desperate.

The feel of his mustache and beard was heady and an interesting stimulant. Sort of a tickle, but not. She hadn't lied, she hadn't ever been kissed by someone with a beard like his...but she found that she liked it. Hell, she flat out liked *him*.

Tony pulled back, resting his forehead against hers. "In case it's not obvious, I want you. No, that's not right. I *need* you, Aimee O'Brien. My first day of work at Gerry Linkous, you shook my hand and looked me right in the eye, welcoming me. You didn't care that I was a man in a female-dominated field. You didn't care that I was a bit scary looking with my long hair and beard. The more time I spent around you, the more I realized what a good person you are." He pulled back to look her in the eyes.

"Then I noticed how you filled out your shirts and pants. The first time you bent over to grab a stray dodgeball, I lost my cool and had to leave so you, and the kids, didn't see exactly how much you affected me. Over and over, you've proved yourself to not only be the kind of person I'd be honored to call my friend, but one I craved with every fiber of my being. Today was the icing on the cake."

"I was scared," Aimee protested, biting her lip.

"So was I. It's a person's actions when they're scared that tell the most about them. Your first thoughts were for the kids. Then me. I chickened out so many times in asking you on a date. But no more. Life's too short. I knew that but didn't act on it, and I could've lost you today. I want you. Not for a quick fuck, but to date. To spend as much time with you as you'll let me. Waking up with your hand on my face was something I'd only dreamed about in the past. Please tell me I have a shot."

Aimee didn't hesitate. "I want that too. You took my breath away that first day. You walked into the room as if you owned it, but not in a conceited way. I saw behind the beard was a good man, one who cared about the students in his class and who wouldn't get bogged down by the politics in the school."

She glanced down, embarrassed, but determined to be honest with him. "I may or may not have dropped things in your presence on purpose."

Tony smiled, his teeth gleaming brightly in the dim light. "Is that right?"

"Uh-huh. I was too embarrassed to make the first move, so I thought maybe if you liked my... assets, you might ask me out. Stupid, huh?"

"No. Not at all. Your assets are definitely liked. In case it's not clear, I'm asking you out now, Aimee. I want to make you breakfast in a few hours, then stick by your side over the next few days as we have to deal with everything that has happened."

"What about at school?"

"What about it?" Tony questioned, sliding his hand under her shirt and resting it on the small of her back.

Aimee shivered at his touch. His hand was warm and when he started caressing her with his thumb, she was lost. She shifted her legs, pushing herself against him in the process. Lord. She forcibly brought her thoughts back to what she was saying. "Do you want to keep our dating a secret when we're at work?"

"Absolutely not." He mock shivered. "You'd let Marci keep hitting on me?"

"No." Aimee's voice was hard and flat. He smiled.

"Exactly. I don't care who knows that we're together. We'll be careful around the kids, but I can tell you right now, several of my students have flat-out told me that I should take you out."

"What? Really? I swear kids are growing up way too fast these days."

"Really. And I agree about leaning too much too fast. But, Aimee, I'm not eighteen. I want to date you with the intention of seeing where it can go. If that means marriage and kids and a dog or two—"

"I'm a cat person," Aimee interrupted him with a smile.

"Excuse me...a dog or two, and a cat...then so be it. I'm not perfect. I'll probably always have to deal with my PTSD, but I think with you by my side, and in my arms, I'll be able to manage it a lot better."

"If Marci hits on you, I'll tear her hair out," Aimee said resolutely, then smiled, ruining the stern countenance she was trying to project. "Make love to me, Tony. Please. I've imagined it in my head so much that I feel like we've done it hundreds of times already."

Tony groaned and pushed his hips up into her stomach. "Lord, Aimee. I'm so hard I'm not going to last. The second I get inside you, I'm gonna lose it."

"That makes me feel better, because I'm so wet right now...listening to you tell me how much you want me only made it worse."

The hand that had been on her back slowly

eased down until he'd pushed under her sweats and undies and was palming her backside. Aimee arched her back, pushing herself up into his touch.

"I do have a perfectly good bed, you know," she teased.

"We aren't going to make it," Tony informed her seriously as Aimee's hand snaked between them and stroked his engorged cock. "Especially if you keep that up," he warned. "I wanted to go slow, to inspect and learn every inch of your body."

"Later," Aimee moaned, as Tony's free hand made its way up the front of her shirt. She leaned up, looking down at the man who she'd wanted for ages, hardly believing that he not only wanted her too, but was interested in a long-term relationship as well. It was like her birthday and Christmas all wrapped into one sexy package.

Shifting suddenly so she was straddling him, Aimee braced herself on his chest and looked down. "I want you, Tony. Here. Now."

"I didn't expect this and I'm not prepared. Condom?"

"I've got a box in my bedroom. If I get up, do you promise not to move?" she asked.

"Not an inch."

Not dragging it out, Aimee eased off of Tony,

and as soon as she cleared his lap, ran into her bedroom and grabbed the box of condoms out of her bedside table. She spared a glance at the expiration date—good, she was still within the safe zone. She'd bought them forever ago, "just in case," and hadn't ever even opened the box.

Racing back into the living room, she saw that Tony hadn't moved at all, except for his hand; he was now stroking himself lazily. He'd popped open the button of his jeans to give himself room and was caressing his cock through his boxers. She moved to the same position she'd been in one minute before and held up the box.

"Not that I expect we'll use them all tonight, but it was faster to bring the whole thing here. They're good for another two months so we're good," she told him, rushing her words together in order to get them out faster. She wanted to get to the good stuff.

Tony didn't say a word, but took the box from her and quickly opened it and took out a strip. He tore one off with his teeth and dropped the rest unheeded to the ground.

He didn't make a fuss out of using the prophylactic, which Aimee appreciated. Leaving the condom between his lips, he moved both hands to her hips and pushed at her sweats. "Lift up," he mumbled around the foil.

Aimee did as he demanded, shivering in anticipation as he pushed her clothes down as far as they'd go while she was still straddled over him. Unless she stood up, or did some acrobatic move to remove the sweat pants, this was going to get interesting.

Keeping one hand at her hip, Tony moved the other between her legs, testing her readiness. She hadn't lied, she was wet. Just the thought that Tony was so anxious to get inside her, and he wasn't taking the time to get to the bedroom or even fully disrobe, did something for her. His thumb pressed over her clit and Aimee thrust her hips toward him without thought.

"Yes, Tony. God, that feels good."

She glanced down and saw that his gaze was fixed between her legs. He couldn't see her clearly because of the dim light, but it was apparent he more than liked what he *could* see…and feel. He hadn't said a word, maybe because he was still holding the condom between his lips, but Aimee thought it was more that he was so far gone in desire for her, he couldn't find the right words.

Aimee writhed on his hand a bit more, feeling

herself get more and more slick as he continued to play with her clit and spread her wetness around. Abruptly he removed his hand and lifted his hips under her, forcing her to sit up straight over him. Tony shoved his own pants and boxers over his hips until his cock bobbed out, and then he ripped open the condom packet.

Smoothing it over his erection, he took hold of Aimee's hips again and helped her move into place over him. It was awkward with her sweats pushed down, and not off, but they were both determined to do this. Now.

"Guide me in," Tony demanded in a guttural voice.

Aimee couldn't remember ever being this turned on. They were both almost fully dressed, their important parts barely revealed. She reached between them and found his hard cock. She caressed it once, cupping his balls at her downward stroke.

"Aimee, I swear to God if you don't quit it, this'll be over before it even begins. Please. Put me in."

Wanting him inside her as much as he apparently wanted to be there, Aimee had mercy on the man. She grabbed his thick erection and scooted forward enough so that the head was nestled between her slick lips. Without waiting for more direction, she pushed her sweats out of the way and slowly eased down, engulfing his hard length into her body.

It was a tight fit, it'd been a while for her, but Aimee didn't stop until he was as far inside her as he could go. She felt her sweats pulling against her legs, and knew she'd have marks when they were done, but at the moment nothing could've forced her to move away from him.

"God," she breathed, the same time that he hissed a breath out between his teeth. "You fit perfectly."

"You are so hot and tight, I can't…I won't…"

Aimee had mercy and moved on him, pulling up so that just the tip was inside her, then easing back down again.

She did this twice before Tony took control. He gripped her waist hard and took over, holding her still while he slammed up and down under her. Aimee moaned and threw her head back, bracing her hands on his thick denim-enclosed thighs behind her, enjoying the thought of Tony Santoro losing control. She remembered her thought from the morning, God, it seemed so long ago, of wanting to see him lose it. She'd just never thought it'd be so soon, and be so fantastically awesome.

"Fucking hell, Aimee, You feel delicious. I can feel you fluttering against me. I can't wait until we can do this bareback."

Aimee didn't know if Tony even knew what words were coming out of his mouth. His teeth were clenched and his head was thrown back. He hadn't closed his eyes though. His gaze remained on her face, which seemed much more intimate than anything she'd done with another man.

They were both still wearing their T-shirts and were mostly dressed, but she felt more naked in this moment than any other time in her life. Tony saw *her*. It was as if he could see her hopes and dreams along with her fears and insecurities. But the thing of it was, that she saw them reflected in his eyes too. He had his own demons. It made her feel as if they could fight them together.

"Yes, Tony. God, you feel good."

"Rub your clit. Take yourself there. I'll do it next time, but show me what you like."

His words were hot and Aimee didn't hesitate. She reached one hand down between her legs and rubbed frantically over her clit as Tony continued holding her still. She felt her orgasm rising, quicker than it ever had before with anyone else. Maybe it was the situation, maybe it had just been too long. Maybe it was the life and death situation she'd faced the day before. But Aimee doubted it. It was Tony.

He was extremely sexy, and after dreaming about him and waiting all those months, he was finally hers.

"I'm coming," she warned Tony, unnecessarily. Her body clamped down on his, and she shuddered over him, putting both hands out to brace herself on his chest.

He didn't say anything, but slammed her down on his cock twice more, as she twitched in his arms, and then held her to him as he reached his own climax. Aimee felt every muscle under her hands tense.

She kept her eyes on his and she swore she had another mini-orgasm at seeing the intense look in his eyes as he came down from his release.

Neither said a word as Tony pulled her down against his chest, keeping them connected for the moment. His hands stroked up her back, under her shirt, lazily.

Finally, he chuckled. "Told you I wasn't going to last."

Aimee giggled. "Yeah, you weren't lying, but you know what?"

"What?"

"It was perfect."

"It was," he agreed.

A full five minutes went by before Aimee spoke again. "As perfect as it was, I can't feel my legs because I think my sweats have cut off my circulation. I have a cramp in my toe and as comfortable as this couch is, I think we need to move this party to my bed."

Tony chuckled under her and kissed her on the temple. "Up you go." He demonstrated his strength by lifting her up and off of him and helping her stand next to him.

Aimee smiled and pulled up her sweats with one hand and laughed as Tony pulled his own pants up as he stood. They walked hand-in-hand to her bedroom, and while he made a trip to her bathroom to take care of business, she whipped off her T-shirt and sweats. She was under the covers by the time Tony came out of the bathroom.

He stripped off his own clothes, completely unselfconsciously, and eased under the covers next to her. Without a word, Tony pulled her to him and she settled herself against his side, using his shoulder as a pillow.

"I know we have a lot to talk about, and while there's nothing I like more than the feel of your naked body next to mine, the only thing I can think about is sleep. Does that make you think I'm less of a man?"

His voice was teasing, but Aimee could hear the undercurrents of worry.

"No. I feel the same. I've gotten myself off imagining what your beard would feel like against my skin, but I'm beat. Tony, we've hopefully got the rest of our lives to be with each other. I'm comfortable and warm and sated. This is perfect."

"You can bet you'll find out what it feels like to have a man with a beard go down on you sooner rather than later. I can't wait to examine every inch of your body…and let you do the same to me. But for now we both need sleep. Relax, Aimee. I've got you."

There were those words again. "I know you do," she whispered against his shoulder. "I know."

The couple fell asleep in each other's arms, neither's demons rearing their ugly heads, making their first night together safe and comfortable. It was the first of many, many nights to come.

EPILOGUE

J ones sighed when the flight touched down. It'd been a crazy couple of days and as happy as he was that he'd been in the right place at the right time in Texas, he was all the more happy to be home. He patiently waited his turn to exit the plane and made his way to the ground floor to grab a taxi.

"Jones."

His name being called surprised him, and he turned. It was his boss. "Hey, Joker. What're you doing here? You headed out on a trip?"

"No. I'm here to pick your ass up."

"Oh, well, thanks. I wasn't expecting it."

"I know, but I gotta stay on top of my game if I'm going to keep ahead of all my employees."

They both laughed. As if Joker had to keep track of them. Every single one of the men and women who worked for him was trustworthy and loyal to a fault.

"Besides, I thought you could use a break. I sent you on what I thought was going to be an easy week away from the hustle and bustle that is our life, and what do you do? End up smack-dab in the middle of the biggest news story to hit the States this month."

Jones chuckled humorously. "Yeah, I don't know how you manage it, boss."

"This time it wasn't me," Joker protested, throwing his hands up in an "I'm not responsible" gesture.

Jones smiled.

Joker's voice got solemn. "Seriously, Jones, you did a good job. I read the transcript of what went down and you did everything right."

"You already read the transcript?" Jones asked incredulously.

"Yeah. Tex sent it to me."

Jones rolled his eyes. "Of course he did. That man is amazing. About the situation…I know we're told not to lie when we talk to the bad guys, but I didn't see any other way to get Bill to hear me. It wasn't as if I could tell him that my parents are still living and we talk on the phone at least once a month…that I grew up in Oak Park, a wealthy suburb of Chicago."

"No, you did exactly right," Joker assured him, clicking the locks on his Highlander as they approached it. "When you're negotiating, you do whatever you have to do, say whatever you need to say to get the hostages out of the situation. You're not there to make friends. Tony and Aimee got out alive. And all the kids." It wasn't a question.

"Yeah."

"Then stop worrying about it."

"I think it was more them than me."

"Bullshit. You let Tony know who you were with that 'quiet professionalism' comment. If you hadn't, he would've had no idea that his brethren were waiting to make their move."

"So he *is* Delta?" Jones asked, settling into the seat. He didn't usually relax when he wasn't the one behind the wheel, but he trusted Joker with his life. He was also very careful with the wording of his question. There was no past tense when it came to Delta Force teams. You might not be actively on a team anymore, but once a Delta, always a Delta.

"Yup. A damn good one," Joker responded matter-of-factly.

"Where are we going?" Jones asked as they went south of the airport instead of north toward his apartment.

"My wife felt bad that you had to work on your semi-vacation, so she told me to pick your ass up and bring you back to the house even if I had to kidnap you. And that's a direct quote, by the way."

Jones grinned. "I can live with that. She make lasagna?"

"Can she make anything else?" Joker mused aloud.

"Don't know, don't care. I could live off that lasagna for the rest of my life."

"And that's why she made it for you." Joker lost his smile and turned to Jones. "Good job, Jones. I'm damn happy to have you on my team."

"My pleasure, Joker. My pleasure."

———

I hope you've enjoyed reading about Annie's favorite teachers. You will officially meet Annie in *Rescuing Emily*, which is the second book in the Delta Force Heroes series.

JOIN my Newsletter and find out about sales, free books, contests and new releases before anyone else!! Click HERE

Want to know when my books go on sale? Follow me on Bookbub HERE!

Would you like Susan's Book Protecting Caroline for FREE?
Click HERE

Also by Susan Stoker

Delta Force Heroes Series

Rescuing Rayne

Rescuing Aimee (novella)

Rescuing Emily

Rescuing Harley

Marrying Emily

Rescuing Kassie

Rescuing Bryn

Rescuing Casey

Rescuing Sadie

Rescuing Wendy

Rescuing Mary (Oct 2018)

Rescuing Macie (April 2019)

Badge of Honor: Texas Heroes Series

Justice for Mackenzie

Justice for Mickie

Justice for Corrie

Justice for Laine (novella)

Shelter for Elizabeth

Justice for Boone

Shelter for Adeline

Shelter for Sophie

Justice for Erin
Justice for Milena
Shelter for Blythe
Justice for Hope (Sept 2018)
Shelter for Quinn (Feb 2019)
Shelter for Koren (June 2019)
Shelter for Penelope (Oct 2019)

SEAL of Protection: Legacy Series

Securing Caite (Jan 2019)
Securing Sidney (May 2019)
Securing Piper (Sept 2019)
Securing Zoey (TBA)
Securing Avery (TBA)
Securing Kalee (TBA)

Ace Security Series

Claiming Grace
Claiming Alexis
Claiming Bailey
Claiming Felicity

Mountain Mercenaries Series

Defending Allye (Aug 2018)
Defending Chloe (Dec 2018)
Defending Morgan (Mar 2019)

Defending Harlow (July 2019)
Defending Everly (TBA)
Defending Zara (TBA)
Defending Raven (TBA)

SEAL of Protection Series
Protecting Caroline
Protecting Alabama
Protecting Fiona
Marrying Caroline (novella)
Protecting Summer
Protecting Cheyenne
Protecting Jessyka
Protecting Julie (novella)
Protecting Melody
Protecting the Future
Protecting Kiera (novella)
Protecting Dakota

Stand Alone
The Guardian Mist
Nature's Rift
A Princess for Cale
A Moment in Time- A Collection of Short Stories
Lambert's Lady

Special Operations Fan Fiction

http://www.stokeraces.com/kindle-worlds.html

Beyond Reality Series

Outback Hearts

Flaming Hearts

Frozen Hearts

Writing as Annie George:

Stepbrother Virgin (erotic novella)

ABOUT THE AUTHOR

New York Times, *USA Today* and *Wall Street Journal* Bestselling Author Susan Stoker has a heart as big as the state of Tennessee where she lives, but this all American girl has also spent the last fourteen years living in Missouri, California, Colorado, Indiana, and Texas. She's married to a retired Army man who now gets to follow *her* around the country.

She debuted her first series in 2014 and quickly followed that up with the SEAL of Protection Series, which solidified her love of writing and creating stories readers can get lost in.

If you enjoyed this book, or any book, please consider leaving a review. It's appreciated by authors more than you'll know.

www.stokeraces.com
susan@stokeraces.com

facebook.com/authorsusanstoker

twitter.com/Susan_Stoker

instagram.com/authorsusanstoker

goodreads.com/SusanStoker

bookbub.com/authors/susan-stoker

amazon.com/author/susanstoker

Made in the USA
Middletown, DE
28 July 2018